Night

of the

Assassin

†

Prequel to the
Assassin series

Russell Blake

First Edition

ISBN: 978-1480238275

Published by

Reprobatio Limited

A NOTE FROM THE AUTHOR

Night of the Assassin is the prequel to *King of Swords*, which chronicles the story of the super-assassin, "*El Rey*" and his plot to execute the presidents of the U.S. and Mexico at the G-20 summit in San Jose del Cabo, Mexico. During the chaotic and breakneck writing of that epic tale, I was constantly struck by fleeting insights into the mind of the killer, some of which I captured in glowing detail in that tome. But even as I put *King of Swords* to bed, I couldn't shake the sense of unfinished business. I'd go to sleep and have vivid dreams, and they were always the same – about the characters in my book. Specifically, they were about the assassin's past. It was like a disease. I couldn't stop thinking about him.

That's unfamiliar to me, for the most part. I had the same general sense when I got done with Al, from *The Geronimo Breach*, but I had no compulsion to write another book about him, fascinating as his character is. I felt closure at the end of that work. I'd told Al's story, as well as I could, and there wasn't more I felt I could add. There were no more words that needed writing.

But I no sooner finished *King of Swords* than I started making notes for a prequel. Which is really the wrong way to go about it. I'm a simple man. When starting a story, I always like the 'Once Upon A Time' part at the beginning, and 'The End' at, well, the end. But that's not how it panned out for me this time. I felt driven to write about the assassin some more, and to delve into his background. What created a man who could dispassionately terminate people's lives for a living? What drove him to do the unthinkable? Was he a monster in the traditional sense?

Did he kick dogs or swerve to hit them in the road? Did he put his socks on before or after his underwear?

It was fascinating to me, because *El Rey* was alive in my head. You see, I knew the answers to the questions I was asking, for once in my life.

And so it came to pass that I have the opportunity to share with you what I gleaned from him. *Night of the Assassin* is a somewhat shorter work, written to flesh out the making of the beast, and is best read as a companion piece after *King of Swords*. It can certainly be read first, but I suspect it will be more satisfying and resonate more if the reader digests *King* first, *Night* second, then the sequels. That's how I envisioned it, but you're free to do as you like. Even if read as a stand-alone or first, *Night* should entertain and satisfy. I'd just recommend it after *King*.

Night of the Assassin is a classic prequel, in that it doesn't repeat information already memorialized in *King of Swords* — so there may be some gaps that don't seem to make sense until both novels are read. *Night*'s purpose, other than to thrill, is to explain, to afford illumination into one of my most fascinating characters yet. *El Rey*'s past, or at least the highlights of it, are alive on the page. If I've done my job right, you'll be hurtled along on a ride like no other, to be at times shocked, titillated, revolted, sad, and ultimately, swept into a dark world of cartel killers and violence, drug deals and paid executions, love and loss.

Enjoy this humble offering, with my compliments.

Your servant,

Russell Blake

CHAPTER 1

Midnight, five years ago, Manzanillo, Mexico

The lights from Contessa, a 160-foot Christensen super yacht, glowed off the calm surface of the harbor below the Grand Bay Hotel in Barra de Navidad, twenty-six miles northwest of Manzanillo – the primary deep water port on the Pacific coast of mainland Mexico. It was a calm spring night, the air heavy with the scent of the ubiquitous tropical flowers, beaded with moisture from the cloudbursts that had sulked over the hazy, humid day. Crickets trilled their mating mantras beneath the broiling heavens, the only sound on the water besides the dull thumping of the disco beat emanating from the massive boat's salon, which lay beneath the superstructure that supported a four-passenger helicopter and a complement of jet skis.

The creaking lines of the yacht strained as the tide rolled in and the moon's perennial pull drew higher the water level in the marina; the heavy ropes that secured the ship to its long concrete dock keened in futile protest.

Armed security men clad in black windbreakers patrolled the concrete walkway that curved the length of the exclusive private marina, the unmistakable outline of Heckler & Koch UMP submachine guns a silent testament to their intent. The battle-hardened men chartered with the safety of those aboard the yacht were dead serious, resonating a constant state of readiness against threats from any approach. The drug cartel skirmishes had escalated over the past two years – the guards had been in some blistering firefights with rival groups and seen more than their share of blood. These were men for whom killing was routine, and they drew their pay with the understanding that any day might be their last.

A radio crackled as the group members checked in with one another, each confirming that all was calm. The routine was to monitor everyone's status at fifteen minute intervals throughout the night. If danger came, it often did so in the wee hours, and the group's leader was keenly sensitive to possible fatigue or boredom – a luxury that could prove fatal on that detail.

Peals of shrill female laughter pierced the night as the salon sliding door opened to allow three scantily clad young Mexican women onto the rear deck, where the ashtrays were located near a well-stocked bar and a sumptuous oversized hot tub. The girls were regular company for the owner of the boat, Sylvio Contreras, the number one warlord in Sonora and the head of the Zapata cartel. Not one was older than nineteen, the youngest seventeen – 'Papi' Contreras liked his meat fresh and tender, the more so since he'd celebrated his fiftieth birthday the prior week. He could certainly afford the best, and there was a constant stream of eager girls interested in exchanging their charms for his largesse; Contreras controlled a significant chunk of the Colombian cocaine and Mexican methamphetamine traffic that made its way through Sonora to the United States, and his annual personal take from the trade exceeded one billion U.S. dollars per year.

Contessa was one of three yachts *Papi* owned – the larger ones were on the eastern shore of Mexico and in Costa Rica, one docked in Cozumel and the other bouncing around Central American ports as its owner's whims dictated. Contessa was more of a weekend getaway destination, a quick hop from home, whereas the others were good for several weeks aboard. *Papi* burned roughly twelve million dollars a year keeping his boats in the water before even starting the engines. They were ready for him at any hour, staffed with full-time crews consisting of captains, chefs, deckhands, mechanics, maids, bartenders and masseuses. Security travelled with him at an extra cost. Then again, *Papi* wasn't price-sensitive, and couldn't have told anyone precisely what he spent on his lifestyle. He knew that his plane had cost forty million, and this boat a hundred and twenty, with the others roughly a quarter billion, but when you were rolling a billion or more bucks a year, what did it matter? The total he'd lavished on toys amounted to what he would clear by June, so it had long ago ceased to have any meaning.

The girls were in high spirits, fueled by a combination of tequila and cocaine, which was one of the other reasons why a place by *Papi*'s side was coveted – you had access to all the high-grade chemical supplementation you could want, in addition to the lavish financial generosity afforded to his female companions. They blew smoke and chatted about clothes and their favorite television programs, taking a break from the *fiesta* that was winding down inside. Contreras had begun his birthday bash several weeks earlier and had decided to make it a month-long event, hopping from destination to destination with his entourage, which consisted of his brother and a group of five or six girls, accompanied by a security detail of two dozen mercenaries. They flew in a 727 he'd acquired for next to nothing when it was put out of service by an American airline and, after ten million in refurbishments at a friend's factory in Costa Rica, it served as his flying army headquarters.

Tensions were high between the Zapatas and the Gulf cartel, as well as the Sinaloa cartel, and the outbreaks of violence had escalated until the death toll reached into the hundreds each month. As with most of the disagreements that resolved in bloody skirmishes, this one had to do with power and money. The Sinaloa cartel felt that Sonora was making too much from its relatively insignificant place in the food chain, and was trying to dis-intermediate Contreras in order to increase its net. The Gulf cartel was more personal – Contreras had butchered the family of one of the Gulf's ranking captains over some real or imagined slight, and that had ignited a blood feud between the two organizations. All of which was just humdrum business for Contreras, who was one of the oldest of the living cartel bosses. He'd invented many of the tactics that were now standard in settling disputes, including beheadings, mass executions with bodies left in prominent places as a warning, the murder of judges and cops, and grenade attacks in densely populated urban areas. Contreras was a maverick in the trade, an innovator, who more than most understood that if you didn't have someone trying to kill you every moment, you were doing something wrong.

Contreras had sent the staff and his brother away to stay the night in the hotel perched above the marina so he could enjoy his debauched party with just his companions. He enjoyed his privacy immensely, even though in his line of work it was a commodity rarer than gold. As a cartel head, he was constantly surrounded by security personnel so part of the appeal of his boats was the ability to enjoy at least the illusion of seclusion.

The door to the salon slid open again and a heavyset hirsute man with a bushy graying moustache and tousled curly black hair, wearing a Versace silk bathrobe and lambskin slippers walked out onto the deck, gesturing to the girls with an unlit Cohiba in his right hand. The youngest, Veronica, leapt to her feet with a lighter and rushed to attend to their host. Contreras smiled at her as he puffed on the hand-rolled Cuban cigar, and playfully slapped one of her perfectly-sculpted buttocks after fondling it through her white mini-booty shorts for a few moments.

"Oh, *Papi*!" she exclaimed with a giggle, faux indignation and petulance dripping from every syllable.

"*Eh*, so how you girls doing? You ready to make a party with your Papi? Come on. You know how I like it," Contreras rasped in his distinctive Sonoran accent.

The girls extinguished their cigarettes and exchanged glances. It was show time. Veronica moved to her two new friends and they began kissing, then caressing each other. Contreras stood by, watching impassively as the action moved from tepid to hot, and clothes began shedding along with any remaining inhibitions. Smooth, creamy-brown skin rubbed against the cushions of the semi-oval exterior seating area, and soon the girls were largely naked, other than a captain's hat the oldest, Ana, kept perched precariously on her head even as Veronica's probing tongue demanded her attention.

Papi opened a small eighteen-carat gold box and quickly tapped out two small piles of white powder on the glass exterior bar behind him. He snorted the heaping lines of cocaine laced with Levitra with gusto as he leered at the *ménage a trois*. He shook his head and stamped his foot against the teak deck in what he imagined resembled a wild bull's mating display before throwing his head back and grinning crookedly at the moon as it struggled to break through the gathered clouds. It was a good life; he was a lucky man. This had been a fantastic birthday so far and whoever had said that life began at fifty wasn't lying. He reached below the bar and extracted a bottle of Herradura Selección Suprema tequila and poured a healthy slug of the amber promise into a tumbler before returning his attention to the nubile entertainment. Yes indeed, a great birthday. He studied the face of his platinum Rolex Masterpiece and noted the time – a little after midnight. Another day older and closer to death. Ah, well. What was one to do? He'd try to enjoy himself nonetheless.

"Ladies. You're shameless. Move inside and let the games begin. And save some love for *Papi*."

The security team studiously avoided looking up at the transom of the huge ship, preferring to scan the periphery for signs of intruders. *Papi's* love for the high life was well known and by now the men had seen everything. It was all fun until he couldn't perform or things turned nasty after too many drugs and the girls ended up begging for forgiveness. They'd had to bury their fair share of young strippers who had failed to judge his moods correctly. He was infamous for being mercurial. A career as a playmate for a *narcotraficante* was a high-risk, high-reward proposition in a world where the men were inured to violence and thought nothing of snuffing out life on virtually any premise, including because it amused them to do so.

A pelican rustled its feathers at the water's edge before taking flight, swooping low over the water as it searched out more tranquil surroundings. Two of the sentries swung around at the sound, ready to engage whatever enemy presented itself. They exhaled with relief when they saw the huge bird lumber into the night air. Everyone's nerves were raw from the prior week's duty, moving from danger zone to danger zone while Contreras partied without a care. They were in friendly territory but that counted for little when he was exposed like this. Every moment held the possibility of an attack by enemies who were every bit as vicious and determined as *Papi*, and when he wasn't in his fortified compound back home, the risk-factor went through the roof.

The men were working in shifts, eight guards each shift, four hours on, eight off, so they could steal some rest and stay alert. After four hours of high-intensity patrolling, acuity fell off markedly and human error became more likely. The cartel game was one where you only got to make one mistake – your last. *Papi* was paying the highest rates in the world for his security; they wanted for nothing, but in return, he expected them to keep him safe no matter what, and if that meant every member of the team taking a bullet for him, so be it.

That was the gig.

The sound of the party from the boat was a headache for them, although no one would dare mention it to *Papi*. But he might as well have painted a big bull's-eye on the super yacht's bow for any hostiles in the area. The head of security, Alberto, clenched his jaw as the women laughed, each squeal of ecstasy an invitation to disaster…in *his* mind. The old pervert ought to restrict banging around with his doped-up teenagers inside the goddamned boat, not out in the open. Why did he need to make such a public display of it? It was recklessly endangering them all. He sucked down his frustration and concentrated on the job at hand, eyes scanning the surrounding dock area and the buildings for any hint of latent danger. They'd be back at Contreras' home compound tomorrow afternoon, and so far there had been no attacks; with any luck they'd make it back without incident, where the routine drill would be executed in a more controlled environment – where they knew everyone and owned the town. This was making him nervous – exposed – on the water, a million miles from nowhere with the boss kite-high on powder and bellowing into the night sky as though he was safe in his own living room.

A cat scurried after a large rat on the slick-wet concrete path by the shops at the far end of the marina, setting Alberto's nerves further on edge. He didn't want to think of how wound-up his men must be after almost ten days of constant vigilance. All he needed was a trigger-happy lapse and they'd have the police and military landing on them, which would be a little awkward given that *Papi* was the number four most wanted man in Mexico. Money obviously bought selective vision where he was concerned, but it would only go so far. Gunfire at a six star hotel's exclusive marina could raise the wrong eyebrows and the last thing Alberto needed was an all-out gun battle with the military in the dead of night.

He silently cursed Contreras for being so careless, then exhaled a sigh of relief when he heard the drug lord call his whores back inside the boat with him. Alberto had six men on land, two on the boat, and one on each side of the bridge superstructure keeping watch for any potential menace that they might miss from the dock. It would be impossible to sneak up on the yacht from the water in the still of the night – a boat would be immediately detected, even if it was being rowed. But he wanted to ensure that all avenues of attack were covered, so even the waterside was being watched. Contessa was docked on a side tie, her port side fastened to the pilings and the starboard side facing the harbor opening, beyond which the bay stretched into a black nothingness. If there was going to be an assault it would have to come from the land because they'd have enough warning from the ship's radar to take positions on the waterside and cut any encroaching vessel to pieces.

They'd covered all possible approaches yet he was still worried. Maybe it was the place, or maybe because it was the last night of *Papi*'s latest binge. But Alberto had an ugly feeling in his guts – and it wasn't something he'd eaten. His primeval senses tingled as if there was something out there coming for them. And whatever it was, it meant them harm.

He called to his men for their radio check-in; everyone responded immediately, sounding alert and precise. They were the best. Seasoned professional killers from a half dozen countries, making thirty-five grand a month each to lay their lives on the line. He didn't like the odds of anyone foolish enough to take them on in the dead of night.

But his gut still told him they had a problem.

The assassin checked the luminescent face of his stopwatch, noting with satisfaction that he was on schedule. He listened for the sound of the party at the marina, which was still some distance away. Faint gusts of music muttered a vague cadence over the water. The target was making it almost too easy for him. Perhaps it was just providence calling time on *Papi*. But whatever the wheels within wheels of cruel nature, he thanked his lucky stars that he'd taken this contract – one of the largest he'd ever been offered, at a million and a half dollars.

He'd planned the attack to the second and researched everything from the marina layout to the surroundings, even going as far as locating blueprints and a schematic for the ship and committing them to memory. This was his specialty – the *impossible to carry-off* execution of untouchables was his stock-in-trade. It had made him infamous in a relatively short time. But this would be the most difficult sanction yet, due to the heightened vigilance of the security team he knew would be on-edge the final night of their rough duty, which concluded in a vulnerable location. He'd thought through all possible ways of terminating Contreras, and when he'd decided on his final plan, even he was impressed at the ingenuity of it. Now he just needed his contractors to be on time and to do their job, and *Papi* was better than dead.

He slipped below the surface of the water and submerged to a depth of fifteen feet. That would be sufficient for his purposes. The small waterproof GPS unit he'd programmed with the coordinates of the dock radiated an orange glow that was readable from three feet away. By his calculations, he would need ten minutes to swim to his starting position before the plan engaged, though he'd allowed himself fifteen, just in case. Better safe than sorry on a night like this. His tank held sufficient air to breathe for an hour, which he hoped would be far more than necessary.

It had been difficult arranging for all the pieces he'd need to end the life of the brutal cartel boss; expensive too, but sometimes cost was key. He'd learned through harsh experience not to pinch pennies or cheap out. By the end of the night he'd be far richer, so in the end, whatever his sunk costs were would have paid for themselves. He was nothing if not pragmatic about the job.

His easy, practiced stroke propelled him smoothly through the warm water as he neared the private marina. He sensed he was close when he felt a current heralding the mouth of the harbor, as the surging tide pulled him through the broad opening.

Visibility was zero in the inky darkness so he was flying entirely by his instruments, which told him he had another hundred and fifty yards to go. Contessa was berthed at the dock closest to the harbor's entrance, commanding the entire length, so there was no cover or alternative to doing the dive. This was the only way to get close.

A commotion from the sea bed startled him with a cloud of muddy sediment. A large stingray rose from the muck and glided by him, nudging his neoprene-encased legs with one of its wings. More sensing the creature than seeing it, he was momentarily caught off guard. His respiration increased as he flailed in alarm, causing a rush of bubbles to hurtle to the surface. Battling for control over his breathing, he struggled to slow his heart rate – after a few seconds of inward composure, he had it back to beating at a moderate pace. He didn't pause long to dwell on the near-miss, beyond musing that it would be ironic if his meticulously plotted assassination fell apart due to surface froth from a panicked brush with a bottom-dwelling *Myliobatoidei*.

Another glance at his watch confirmed that he still had five minutes to go. By his reckoning he should be sixty or so yards from the front of the boat, and ninety from his targeted position. After a few more moments of swimming, he dimly registered the hull of the massive ship above him – an opaque outline floating on an already dark surface, faintly illuminated by lambent swirls of the surrounding marina lights. Carefully calculating the distance, he moved to the spot his schematics told him would be the correct one for his purposes.

From a mesh sack attached to his dive belt, he fished out a suction cup with a handle on one end, which he affixed to the hull. The assassin could feel the vibration of the big generators that provided all the power when the massive twin MTU turbo-diesels were at rest. As expected, all systems were operating at full bore on the luxurious yacht. He extracted a waterproof battery-powered drill, and after taking one final confirming look at his position on the hull, he jammed the bit against the fiberglass and depressed the trigger. The diamond-tipped steel shredded its way through hard, fibrous material – almost five inches thick. The bit was six. Two minutes later he was through. He dropped the drill back into his sack and extracted a small gas canister with a rotating valve on the end, where it connected to a custom-fabricated seven-inch tube that would be a snug fit in the hole. He jammed it up into the new opening and twisted the valve, wishing he could hear the satisfying hiss that would terminate the target.

Hopefully.

That was where part two of the plan came in.

The assassin depressed a button on the suction cup and it dropped away from the hull. He swam to the far side of the ship that was facing the bay and cautiously poked his head out of the water, right next to the section where the engine vents drew in air. Another glance at his watch confirmed that he had a hundred and forty more seconds before it was show time. He groped in the sack and, after re-submerging, drilled another hole, this time where the central air conditioning units were situated. He repeated the procedure with a second gas canister and returned to the surface again, hurriedly extending a telescopic tube akin to a car radio antenna. The assassin fitted a third, larger canister onto the end of the extension and, now in position and prepared, waited for the fireworks to begin.

Alberto was the first to hear the big chopper's rotors. By the time he had radioed to his men, the sound of the aircraft had increased to a chattering roar. A searchlight stabbed through the night, racing over the buildings and then towards the marina, tracing over the assembled boats until it finally alighted on Contessa's towering mass, blinding the two armed sentries in the top-level bridge. Alberto screamed into the radio to his men to hold their fire – nobody from the helicopter was shooting. The piercing light slowly moved along the concrete path, locking onto the armed men and freezing each in place before it moved on to the next. Eventually, satisfied that there was no unusual mischief going on at the marina, the beam shut off and the chopper rose, hovering for another twenty seconds before banking and moving back towards its home base in Manzanillo.

Alberto swore to himself. That had been way too close. It was one of the navy copters, no doubt sent over to check on reports of armed men on the waterfront. The army and the navy chiefs in the area had been paid off, so there shouldn't have been any problem. It likely took a couple of radio exchanges before they called off the dogs. Few things in life scared Alberto, but the prospect of taking on a contingent of armed Mexican marines was one of them; the army wasn't a problem, but the marines knew their shit. They were the equivalent of the American green berets, the toughest of the tough, and they generally meant business. Alberto should know: he employed three ex-marines who were genuine, authentic hard cases – even in a world where blood was spilled casually on a daily basis.

The unexpected fire-drill over, the patrols commenced again. Everything returned to a fragile calm. The night was still, and Contessa gently rocked against the swell of the incoming tide, the music from within still booming its siren song into the deep.

The assassin made his way through the cabin to the main stateroom, his silenced pistol at the ready. He'd brought it in a waterproof bag, in which he kept anything that shouldn't get immersed during the dive. He didn't think he'd need to use it, but better to be prepared. He'd pulled his flippers off and set them on the rear deck, where he could grab them in a hurry. Worst case, he could always swim without them, although it would be much rougher going. That wasn't his most pressing problem now, though. He needed to memorialize his success and get the proof back to his clients so he could collect the second half of his fee – and build his reputation in the process.

He pushed the door to the master stateroom open and encountered a tableaux straight out of hell. *Papi* lay naked in the center of the bed, surrounded by his three young playmates, also naked. All were dead. The nerve gas he'd bought from the Russians had done its work, circulating via the three zoned air conditioners. He'd been guaranteed that the gas would kill within ten seconds of inhalation, but he needed to be sure. That's what made him who he was. He was the man who made sure.

The sight of the female corpses, bloody foam caked around their mouths and noses, already cyanotic, had no effect on him. This was his job, his chosen profession. Collateral damage was regrettable, but part of the deal. The girls would have likely been dead within a few years anyway, either at the hands of these goons…or their rivals. It was a fast money life, which didn't come with a retirement plan.

Breathing through his respirator, the assassin studied the dead cartel boss, then fired a single shot through his forehead, more for effect than anything. He inspected his handiwork dispassionately before reaching into the watertight gun bag for a cell phone and a laminated rectangle. Approaching the man, he positioned the card almost tenderly on his exposed throat before snapping a photo with the phone. The figure on the card seemed to watch the proceedings without interest, his medieval regal gaze unblinking in perpetuity, the double-edged blade of his clutched sword forever pointing at the heavens. Satisfied with his handiwork, the assassin dropped the phone back into the sack and sealed it before placing it into the web bag hanging from his dive belt.

A noise from above jolted him. He heard movement from up on the bridge – heavy footsteps that carried down into the mid-ship stateroom, which could signal either a problem or a shift change. The one part of the plan he hadn't been able to nail was a detailed agenda for the security team. There was just nobody he could find that could be paid off, so he'd had to wing it. He hoped that wasn't a fatal flaw tonight. He'd know soon enough; even though his work was done, he still needed to complete phase two of the sanction, which was often the hardest part – the part where he got out alive.

Alberto called his men to an area near the dock and briefed the new arrivals. They would be on shift until four-twenty, at which point they'd be relieved by a new, fresh set of eight. The men handed the replacements their weapons and spare clips, then moved in a group toward the hotel, a wing of which had been booked for the security detail and boat staff. Alberto debated going with them, having already been on for eight hours, but he couldn't eradicate the twisting in his stomach that something was amiss, so he knew there was no way he'd be able to sleep. He held up a pair of night vision goggles and studied the rocks of the jetty that protected the harbor, slowly and carefully scanning every foot of them.

Nothing.

A cry from the bridge interrupted his reconnaissance, and he looked up to where one of the new arrivals was waving. *What an idiot. Why didn't he use the radio? That's what they were for.*

Alberto turned the volume up on his handheld and called to the man. "What is it?"

"I...was *Papi* or any of the girls swimming earlier today or this evening? I've been gone for eight hours."

"No. I don't think so. Why?" Alberto asked, honestly puzzled by the question.

"There's a pair of—"

Without warning the radio went dead. The hair on Alberto's arms stood up as he peered through the goggles up at the bridge. He couldn't see either of the men who were stationed there as sentries.

"Bridge. Come in. Repeat. Come in. Do you read me?" Alberto hissed into the radio, his hopes sinking even as he called.

The body of one of the two guards sailed over the side of the bridge, landing in a formless mass four stories below on the concrete surface of the dock near Alberto's feet. Alberto stared at the body in disbelief, a stain of thick, dark blood quickly pooling around the corpse. Moments later a second corpse hurtled over – the security men all rushed toward the yacht, now in full-scale attack mode. The two men on the bridge had been in unassailable positions, with the only access from the rear deck...and the salon, where *Papi* had last been seen leading his friends below to his palatial zebra wood-paneled stateroom.

The night abruptly exploded into an inferno, temporarily blinding Alberto. From inside the boat, the *whump* of an incendiary grenade illuminated the interior with a white-hot flash before the ensuing blaze erupted from the side windows, shattered from the scorching blast. A figure in black wearing scuba gear swung from the bridge over the waterside of the ship, dropping the forty feet into the harbor even as Alberto hazily trained his weapon on him and opened fire with a hail of bullets. Burst after burst of sizzling lead seared into the water where the diver had submerged, and Alberto's men quickly joined him, shooting point blank into the surface in the hopes of hitting something.

The assassin allowed himself to sink to the bottom, twenty-five feet below the surface. He kicked a few feet and took cover beneath the gargantuan hull, the bullets tearing harmlessly through the deep where he would have been if he was stupid enough to try to swim out of the harbor's mouth. He'd give it a few minutes and let the gunmen exhaust their wrath before doing so – he still had sufficient air. Even the most dedicated mercenaries would tire of emptying weapons into the bay for no reason, so it would only be a few more moments before they stopped and began thinking about evacuating before the military arrived to check on the blaze.

It would be a long slog across the bay without the swim fins he'd been forced to leave on the aft deck. That was regrettable. He made a mental note in the future to bring an extra set with him to attach to the hull, where they would be safely waiting for him if he was forced to make a hasty departure. He checked his watch and peered through the gloom at his regulator gauge, which he illuminated using the dim glow from the GPS. He had forty-five percent left, which would get him out of the harbor and at least halfway across the bay before he needed to jettison the tank and switch to using his snorkel.

With any luck at all he would be on the far side, on the banks of the little fishing hamlet of Barra de Navidad, within an hour and fifteen minutes, where a battered Toyota Tacoma sat waiting on a dark, deserted street by the water. It would be the least-expected escape route given it was the farthest point from the ship. If the security detail still had any fight left in them after losing their meal ticket, they'd deploy to the more obvious areas closer to the yacht, although any pursuit would be hurried due to concerns over the arrival of the marines. The odds of there being any serious hunt for him were about zero, he knew. They'd be far more interested in clearing out before they had to explain their heavily armed presence to the military.

From the town of Barra, he could be in Manzanillo within forty minutes, or better yet, at one of the big hotels just north of town. They were showing their age, but he still liked Las Hadras resort as a place to lay low for a few days while waiting for the wire transfer to hit his account. When he got to shore he would e-mail the photo of *Papi*, with his distinctive calling card in glorious display, using his cell phone's internet capability. The client would be suitably impressed, given yet another impossible execution in his notorious string of accomplishments had gone off without a hitch.

The gas had been a novel touch and he'd been delighted with the results. It was short-duration and would have blown off within five minutes of entering the air-filtration and conditioning system, so the only trace any investigators would find would be the empty canisters wedged into the hull. At that stage it would be pretty obvious that something in the atmosphere had killed the passengers, so the discovery would have zero effect on anything. The vendor had done well with the choice; the assassin grinned behind the heavy glass mask – he'd use him again. Reliability in the assassin's game was key to sustaining rewarding long-term relationships.

Rousing himself from his reverie, he began swimming slowly away from the boat, hugging the bottom so as to avoid any telltales to the flashlight beams playing across the surface. They were wasting their time but he wanted to take no further chances. He resolved to hold his breath for the two minutes it would take to make it to the harbor entrance and to safety – there was no point in increasing the odds of more shooting by leaving an unnecessary bubble trail up top if he didn't have to.

By the time the flames were extinguished there was little left of the ship's upper salon or staterooms, other than the main bedroom used by the owner. When Alberto made his way down the shattered stairs to the companionway that led to that area, he already knew in his heart what his eyes would confirm. His boss, his sacred charge, was dead. Still, nothing could have prepared him for the vision of a naked *Papi* with the tarot card sticking out of his bloody, froth-caked mouth, surrounded by the cold-blue naked flesh of his nubile companions who had obviously died in excruciating agony. His blood ran cold when he saw the image of the seated regent protruding from *Papi*'s face. He'd heard the stories, the rumors of the ghost that came to kill, but had never believed they were true.

Until now.

Until he'd witnessed the handiwork with his own eyes – the handiwork of the King of Swords, or *El Rey* as he was known in Mexico. He was every heavily protected target's worst nightmare – the man who could walk through walls or up the sides of buildings, and from whom no one was safe. Seeing the assassin's calling card was a loss of any innocence or hope he'd ever had. Because now, Alberto knew that there was indeed a boogeyman, a devil that danced in the darkness, a stealer of things precious for delivery to hell.

Alberto could say with assurance that there was something that scared him more than the Mexican marines, more than torture, more than the prospect of death itself. He, a man for whom slaughter and killing was mundane, had seen the face of true evil, and it had stared back at him, unflinching.

El Rey had come during the night and stolen *Papi*'s soul.

CHAPTER 2

Twenty-five years ago, Sinaloa, Mexico

The flames leapt up into the night sky, their eerie flickering the only evidence that anything man-made had existed in the deserted field of marijuana plants. The shacks were ablaze, sending embers shooting into the air as they carried the captives' hopes of survival to heaven with them.

The little girl sobbed, terrified of what was to come. Her mother, helpless beside her, howled an incoherent, primal sound into the ground next to the mutilated corpse of her youngest, while futilely struggling against the crude plastic ties that bound her bloody wrists. This had been the worst night in the toddler's short, harsh life, and it seemed surreal to her. She hoped it was a nightmare. The dead form of her father lay sprawled next to her mother, his life extinguished in an unspeakable manner. She didn't understand any of it. She wanted to live. She had so much to do – her life was just starting.

True, it had been a difficult existence so far, as the daughter of a dirt-poor farmer in the hills of rural Mexico; another mouth to feed in a hard environment where money was non-existent and the family lived off the land. But, as with most children, she loved her parents wholeheartedly, no matter what the circumstance; they were her universe – and she had just begun viewing the world as a thing apart from them.

As the seasons came and went, the family's time was spent working their meager patch of land: a plot of several acres that had been in the family for over a century. They survived without any creature comforts, their power provided by an ancient gas-powered generator which was used only in emergencies – gasoline being far too precious a commodity to waste on luxuries such as lights. There was no plumbing; their water came from an artesian well. Still, it was a life, her life, and the only one she'd known in her four years on the planet – and like most organisms, she wanted it to continue as long as possible.

Then the unthinkable had happened. The men had arrived in their huge truck, and soon the shack the little family called home was ablaze and her sister and father were no longer of this world. And now she knelt, crying while she murmured the only prayer she knew, hoping it would work as a talisman to keep the bad men at bay.

"Our Father, who arth in heaven...," she lisped in a soft, tremulous tone.

She swiveled her head and watched as an older man, who had just arrived after their field had been set alight, walked slowly back to his vehicle holding the hand of a young boy – her brother.

One of the remaining two men moved beside her and grabbed her mother's hair, lifting her to her knees, her grief shrieking in gasping sobs even as she trembled in shock and fear. Her shoulders shook the shabby sleeves of her torn peasant dress, now bloody and filthy from the abuse she'd received at the hands of the animals who stood by them with their pistols and cowboy boots. A gunshot rang out, deafening the little girl – her mother fell forward onto the bloody dirt, her suffering ended, gone to join her husband and baby. The little girl cried to the silent god who had abandoned her, an innocent, even as she continued to recite the words she'd been assured would protect her through anything.

"Thy king done come…"

She closed her eyes against the horror of the scene and imagined a place where she would be forever young, playing in a beautiful grass field with puppies and ponies; her father, young, healthy and vibrant running beside her as her mother tossed her baby sister into the air, eliciting squeals of glee from the delighted tike. She sensed the cold menace of the gun barrel against the back of her tiny head, and redoubled her efforts to send her *m'aidez* to her creator.

"Thy will be—"

The lead ripped through her cerebrum, abruptly terminating her brief sojourn on earth. Her frail body tumbled lifelessly to the ground.

For her, the ordeal was over.

The men watched as the cannabis caught fire, fed by the gasoline that had been so frugally saved for the family's power, their butchery merely another day's work in their brutal world of enforcement of their absolute power. Both would sleep well that night, their consciences long ago having been discarded as impediments to their working for the group that would later become the Sinaloa cartel – the most powerful and ruthless of the Mexican *narcotraficantes*. The night's drama had been another in a long line of horrors they'd inflicted on their fellow men in order to solidify their *jefe*'s control over the region. The citizenry only understood and respected one thing, and that was brute force. They were the delivery system for that primal justice, and they knew that nobody would ever miss the peasant family or question the events of that night. It was all business as usual; nobody wanted to have the men visit their home if they were too inquisitive about what had happened or where the farmer and his family had gone. The events would remain just another footnote in the slaughter that was an ongoing part of the drug traffic in Mexico. There was nobody to defend the innocents, and so they perished, as countless others had before them in brutal episodes that determined nothing. Mexico's soil was steeped in the blood of the helpless – the men knew that nobody would mourn them. They had no power, no clout, and so were disposable.

The enforcers returned to their truck, which started with a roar, and they tore off into the night, down the dirt track that led to civilization, such as it was.

∂∙∾

Twenty years ago, Sinaloa, Mexico

Horses whinnied as they galloped around the periphery of the open field. The men gathered in the center whistling at the ponies as they celebrated their temporary equestrian freedom. A sprawling mission-style hacienda sat imposingly in the distance – easily twenty-thousand feet of interior space built on a bluff overlooking a river which burbled softly below it as it carried fresh water from the mountains, so vital for the irrigation of the region's crops, which were mainly tomatoes and marijuana.

The majority of the cannabis grown in Mexico came from Sinaloa, and it had been this harvest that had been instrumental in the creation of the modern cartel system. Originally, only a few families engaged in the trafficking of marijuana to the U.S., along with heroin of moderate quality and purity produced in modest, local fields. It had been a small business, operated like a cottage industry, tightly held with a minimum of violence other than turf wars over growing and distribution rights.

Then, in the late 1970s, the dynamics had shifted; the smuggling networks that had been engaged in this relatively benign trade took on the burden of moving cocaine through Mexico for the Colombian cartels, and then the money got much bigger as the Cali and Medellin cartels grew increasingly reliant on their Mexican smugglers to get the product to the U.S. This naturally led to a situation where the Mexicans began getting paid in product, versus cash, driving them to become distributors, as opposed to transporters – and the money involved took another quantum jump. By the early 1990s, the Mexican cartels were handling much of the trafficking for the Colombians, whose cartels had disintegrated in the late 1980s with their survivors now focused mainly on manufacturing.

Within a little over a decade, a small business had become a multi-billion-dollar industry and the various factions fought it out for the rights to their geographical areas. By 1990, the Sinaloa cartel was the most powerful in all Mexico – in all the world, in fact – primarily because the 'Godfather' of the Mexican drug trade, Miguel Angel Félix Gallardo, was from Culiacan, the capital of Sinaloa. It was he who ran a hundred percent of the trade through Mexico during the Seventies and Eighties, and he who had the relationships with the Colombians. In the mid-Eighties, he decided to divide up Mexico into regions, so the power that was naturally concentrated in Sinaloa remained there, with the other cartels acting as satellites to that main central group.

That changed when Gallardo went to prison in the late Eighties, which created a vacuum in the leadership and opened the door for the smaller, less important cartels to assert a better foothold. In particular, the Tijuana cartel and the Juarez cartel had jockeyed for greater sway and a larger chunk of the profits, leading to often bloody wars with their Sinaloa brethren.

The group of men watching the horses laughed easily together, cans of Tecate tempering the worst of the mid-day heat. It was fall, the storm season was largely over, but the temperatures could still reach the high nineties during the day, bringing with it substantial humidity. The oldest of the men, *Don* Miguel Lopez, a tall, lean man with the leathery complexion that came from a lifetime outdoors, had his left hand resting on the shoulder of a ten-year-old boy, already lanky from the summer's growth spurt that had left him all arms and legs, an alien in an unfamiliar body. It was his birthday and, at ten, it was time for him to begin learning the skills he'd require to survive in an ever-competitive world. In Mexico, with a head of the household who was one of the original ranking members of the Sinaloa cartel, that translated into more than reading, writing and arithmetic. *Don* Miguel, the elder statesman of the group, smoothed his mustache and lifted his cowboy hat, wiping away the sweat from his brow with a soiled red cloth handkerchief he carried for that purpose, and then patted the boy's shoulder.

"It's time for you to learn about the way of the world. As part of your birthday, I'm handing you over to Emilio here, who will teach you everything you'll need to know about maintaining a healthy body and mind, as well as about horses and weapons. And who knows; maybe when you're older, he can even teach you a thing or two about women," *Don* Miguel joked. The surrounding men obligingly laughed at his playful sense of fun. "My business will be demanding an increasing amount of my time and I'll be traveling much of the year, so I'm entrusting you to Emilio's capable hands. You're to treat him with the same respect you would afford me. Are we clear on that? He's your mentor, which is a position of honor, but it's also one of responsibility, and if you fail to apply yourself it will reflect poorly on him."

The boy nodded his understanding. He didn't talk much – had never seen much point to it. Even at his tender age he'd discovered that it wasn't what people said, it was what they did that counted, so engaging in what he viewed as meaningless banter served no purpose. He looked up at Emilio's wizened face, battered by the cruel vagaries of a fickle universe, and fixed the man with his gaze – remarkable in its intensity, especially given that he was just a boy.

Emilio regarded him and then grunted, gesturing with his head for the boy to follow him. The pair walked toward the stables and, once out of view of the men, Emilio got down on one knee so as better to get his point across.

"My job is to make you a man. I know your history, and I'm here to tell you nothing matters but the present and the future. Where you've been? That's meaningless. Nobody cares. The only reason the past matters is so you can learn from it. That's the whole reason making mistakes and surviving them matters. Experience is what we call the mistakes we survive." Emilio grinned, and tussled the boy's hair. "And I've got a lot of experience. So you're going to stick with me, *eh*? Every day, before you go to school, we will spend an hour together learning how to discipline your body. Every afternoon after school, you'll spend three hours with me, learning how to discipline your mind. Once you have both under total control, we'll proceed to the fun stuff – learning how to shoot, ride, swim, hunt, and how to stay hidden. But I can't teach you anything until you have control over yourself."

The boy glared at him dubiously, his dislike of the situation and his new mentor obvious. Emilio swatted him on the side of the head, just enough to get his attention.

"You see? You don't have control. You can't hide your emotions, so you're an open book to anyone who wants to read you. You don't like me, and it's obvious – so I now have power over you. You've given me that power by failing to contain your feelings, and I can use it to hurt you. So your first lesson is to control your emotions. If not, they'll control you, and you'll be blown around like a leaf, always reacting to whatever storm is taking place in your brain."

Even at ten years old, the boy had learned to listen. Emilio could see the wheels turning in his small head as he absorbed what the older man had said.

"It doesn't matter to me whether we do this the easy way or the hard way. Either will work. If you're interested in proving you're stubborn, save your energy for something that matters. You want to prove something, show me you're determined; you'll have plenty of chances. My job is to build you into a leader, a man others will look up to, who makes smart decisions with a level head, and who never, ever loses his cool. You'll soon figure out that it's better to put some effort into learning what I'm teaching rather than fighting it. In the end, resisting the lessons will just be delaying the inevitable, which is getting to the fun parts. So decide. Make a choice, then eliminate all other possible outcomes. That will be your road. I hope you select a good one," Emilio concluded, and then opened the barn door and moved inside to the bales of hay. He studied the pile and motioned with his hand to the old pitchfork leaning against the far wall.

"Happy birthday. Starting today, and every day until I tell you that you can stop, I want you to move the hay from these bales, over to this pile by the feeding trough. Spend one hour per day doing it, every morning before school." Emilio glanced at the boy, who now regarded him impassively. The old man reached into his pocket, and produced a new stainless steel wrist watch, tearing off the tags as he examined the clasp. He looked at the time and then tossed it to the boy, who snatched it out of the air with ease.

"That's my birthday gift to you. It's always important to give, in order to get. I see you're right-handed by your catch. That can be a liability over time. We'll work together so that you can do any task with either hand, equally comfortably. If you're ever wounded in one arm, you can use the other, and that edge could be the difference between you living or dying on the floor. Everything I do has a reason. But for now, start on the hay. Do you know how to read a clock? How to tell time on that watch?"

The boy nodded his head in the affirmative.

"Another lesson. Never tell me you know something if you don't. I don't mind it if you don't know – not knowing if you haven't been shown isn't your fault. Not knowing because you weren't shown because you pretended to know...that's stupidity," Emilio cautioned.

"I know how to tell time; how to read a clock. I'm not stupid," the boy declared angrily.

"Ah, so he speaks. Very good. But you still haven't learned my first lesson. By showing me how you're feeling, either with your voice, or eyes, or body, you're giving me an advantage over you. And I can use that to destroy you. So we'll work on you learning to control your emotions, to be cool and collected at all times. It's the first lesson I'll teach you, and probably the single most valuable." Emilio studied the boy's features, the dark brown eyes radiating a quiet intensity. "Once you master the ability to manage your inner domain, you will have power over others, instead of them having power over you. Learning to do so is a matter of practice. The more you practice, the more composed you'll become, and the faster you'll progress. It's not just about hiding your emotions from others – it's about arresting your state. If you lose control, you lose. It's that simple. If nothing else, always remember that. You lose." Emilio glanced at the pitchfork, then back at the boy.

"And something tells me you don't like losing, *eh*? Well, here's another piece of experience from a lifetime of mistakes: winning takes work – usually a lot of it. And practice. And commitment. Which is where I come in. So, happy birthday, treat your watch with care and it will function well for many years – and get to the hay – it's not going to move itself."

Emilio turned and strode out of the building and onto the dirt riding path, leaving the boy to his thoughts.

Emilio could tell he was one tough little bastard, that was for sure. It wouldn't be easy reining him in. It was the same with the horses. You had to break their spirits sufficiently so that they could learn how to behave in a productive manner, but not crush them entirely – you wanted a thoroughbred that desired to win…or it became a plow horse. *Don* Miguel was a smart man, and he had been clear that he expected the boy groomed to be a suitable heir to his rapidly expanding fortune. The next five or six years would be the ones that forged the boy's character and made him into whatever he would ultimately be. Tough was good. So was stubborn. And smart. *Don* Miguel had stressed how intelligent the boy was, devouring every book he could get his hands on. That could be a powerful combination of character traits. Emilio would steer him in a direction where he had an outlet for his obvious simmering anger.

The *Don* didn't have time to raise him and teach him what he'd need to know. Every day brought more and more threats to the *Don*'s survival; the truth was, he would be in hiding much of the time, directing his affairs from a safe distance. *Don* Miguel was now a major player in the Mexican trafficking scheme, but with the spoils came the risks. There was a constant and never-ending supply of enemies who would cut his throat for the slightest advantage. The danger was very real and immediate. So he would leave his beloved *estancia*, his horses, and become a general in the ongoing war, coming home only for brief visits when he deemed it to be safe. It was an unforgiving existence that could end at any moment, but it was the life he'd chosen, and now he ran things in much of northern Sinaloa – he was becoming a fabulously wealthy man, even by cartel standards.

In the *Don*'s business, there was no retiring, no quitting to pursue other interests. The trade operated according to the law of the jungle: you kept killing until something killed you. If you were the meanest and smartest predator, perhaps you'd have a long life. So far, *Don* Miguel had proved to be up to every challenge. That could change in a blink, but Emilio didn't think so. He was one in a million; easily a genius, as well as utterly ruthless and clinically calculating. That combination of traits was rare, especially in a business that boasted more testosterone than a boxing club.

But the *Don* was also looking to the future. He realized that the boy would always be a target, no matter what pursuit he chose as an adult. Which meant that he needed to be equipped with skills that would enable him to survive in a world filled with enemies. Even if he didn't become a predator himself, he would need to learn the lessons that would keep him from showing his soft underbelly to those that would cheerfully rip out his entrails.

Emilio was the boy's best shot at survival. He would teach him the lessons he would need to learn well in order to stay alive, and hopefully to flourish.

He would make the boy into a man.

Starting today.

CHAPTER 3

Sixteen years ago, Sinaloa, Mexico

The boy had grown considerably over the thousand days since Emilio had taken over his care, and had mastered all of the tasks he'd been assigned. He was remarkably self-possessed, excelled in his studies, and had worked diligently on his exercises. Emilio had transitioned him from hay to a real workout, in order to keep up with his rapidly developing physique. His upper body was sculpted by a series of isometric exercises, culminating in chin-ups and push-ups; his lower body was conditioned with increasingly longer runs. Even as he approached his fourteenth birthday, he could easily be mistaken for two years older and his gait had taken on the measured confidence of an athlete.

Don Miguel had occasionally stopped by – and each time he'd been surprised by the boy's development. Gone for six months at a time, it seemed that with each visit, the boy was a few inches taller and sporting a few more pounds of muscle. *Don* Miguel was pleased with the metamorphosis and indicated his satisfaction with generous increases in the boy's allowance, as well as in Emilio's remuneration. The boy was now easily half of Emilio's workload because the number of skills to be learned increased with his age. He was already an accomplished horseback rider and swimmer, and had shown considerable aptitude for archery. It wasn't unusual for the boy to spend hours each day patiently firing at targets with his hunting bow, gradually increasing the distance as he mastered a given range. That was how he approached things – methodically, analytically. He'd quickly taken Emilio's counsel to heart and worked at controlling his emotions no matter what the stimuli. Emilio had taught him any number of tricks to help him remain detached and calm in any situation.

On his fourteenth birthday, *Don* Miguel was nowhere to be found, but had sent a substantial financial stipend to be lavished on the boy's newest tier of training – weapons. Emilio had received instructions to teach him to become proficient with handguns and rifles, and had sourced a variety of guns of all shapes and sizes. By this point, he knew the boy would practice until he excelled at whatever the challenge was – and he wasn't disappointed with his firearms progress. Within a year, the boy was a crack shot with any weapon you handed him, firing either right or left handed. He'd become ambidextrous through discipline and application, and spent three to four hours every afternoon at the private shooting range Emilio and he had constructed for his use.

Firearms were illegal in Mexico, but out in the country, with no neighbors for miles and with all the local police on the payroll, nobody seemed to mind the constant volleys of shots that echoed through the trees for hours on end. Nobody was being hurt, no harm was done and everyone was getting bountiful Christmas bonuses each year, so there was no reason to rock any boats. It was live and let live as far as law enforcement was concerned, which worked out in everyone's best interests.

The boy quickly grew comfortable with any guns provided to him. As his fourteenth year transitioned into his fifteenth, he was exceeding all expectations Emilio had of him. One afternoon, shortly after the boy's fifteenth birthday, Emilio performed the ultimate pistol test, bringing with him a Smith and Wesson .357 Magnum revolver and a Ruger 9mm semi-automatic. He set up two coffee cans thirty yards away from each other, paced off forty yards with the boy and held out both handguns.

"The target on the left, shoot with your left hand using the revolver. The one on the right, use the Ruger. Fire as quickly as you can while maintaining accuracy," Emilio instructed.

The boy hefted both pistols, getting a feel for their weight. He knew from hundreds of hours of experience that firing a big bore revolver required different skills than a smaller caliber automatic. Besides the difference in recoil, which was considerable and had to be adjusted for, a revolver used each trigger pull to rotate the cylinder that held the bullets, requiring significantly more pressure and causing a reflex that would make most shooters fire high, pulling up from the target. Firing a revolver with both hands in a military crouch was hard enough, but doing so with his 'weak' hand while adjusting for the low recoil of the Ruger was an almost impossible challenge.

"How many pounds of trigger pressure on the Ruger?" the boy asked.

"I wonder, if you're in a situation where you have to use someone else's weapon, whether they'll be able to answer that for you? My guess is, not," Emilio replied.

The boy shrugged. Never hurt to ask.

He calculated the distance and then began firing, alternating weapons, rapidly, but not in an uncontrolled manner. The pair of cans, which they'd filled with water, sprouted leaks. After emptying both weapons in their direction they walked over to inspect the results.

Of six possible hits from the revolver, five had found their mark. All nine that Emilio had loaded the Ruger with found theirs.

"*Heh.* Not bad. I would have guessed you wouldn't have hit any with the revolver. The only problem is that the one you didn't hit it with might have been the one you needed to save your life. We'll need to practice this more, switch things up on you. And I want to start practicing shooting while running or riding in a vehicle soon. Once you master being able to hit anything using whatever you're handed from a still position, we'll kick it up a notch and have you simulate real combat situations where you're not stationary." This was high praise from Emilio, who was grudging with his accolades.

The boy smiled. He understood his performance was extraordinary. Nobody he knew could have done it. But Emilio was right. There was no room for error, and no satisfaction to be had from being almost great.

Emilio's only concern as the boy matured was the inevitable interest that he showed toward his daughter, Jasmine. She was a year younger than the boy but already a beauty, thankfully reflecting her mother's genes rather than Emilio's. Also highly intelligent, she was every bit the boy's match when it came to anything intellectual, and there had been a simmering kind of sibling rivalry between them since they'd first met.

Jasmine's mother had died when she was five, leaving Emilio to shoulder the burden of raising her, assisted by his sister and mother. One of the benefits of being a breadwinner of secure means with a generous employer like *Don* Miguel was that you could help support family members, and Emilio did his fair share. In return for which, the ladies, as he called them, raised Jasmine while he was working. It wasn't a perfect situation but it had done well enough by her and she'd blossomed into a gorgeous, charming example of classical Mexican beauty, all gleaming black hair, white teeth and coffee-kissed skin.

The only quirk she'd shown was a deep interest in the occult, driven no doubt by a frustrated desire to somehow relate to her departed mother. She was Catholic, of course, as was everyone in Sinaloa they knew, but she'd grown restive with the faith and had taken to reading tomes of dubious virtue, on divining, and psychic powers, levitation and transmutation, and all manner of arcane, esoteric disciplines. Jasmine had of late been sneaking out and spending time with an old woman who claimed to read fortunes in one's palm, as well as through studying tea leaves – all for a price, of course. Emilio had been worried, but the ladies had assured him that it was just a phase; a way to appear more mysterious as she came of age. He'd never understood women, having found them all equally inscrutable and impossible to read, so in the end he'd decided to take the advice of his mother and sister and let the fascination run its course.

Emilio's days consisted of working with the boy and the horses. Once both children were home from school, his attention focused almost exclusively on the boy, leaving Jasmine to be trained by the ladies in the feminine ways of the world. This wasn't because of any lack of love on Emilio's part. On the contrary, he lived for Jasmine. It was just that as she'd grown from a child into an adolescent he'd felt out of his depth, and now that she was thirteen, and moody, her body sprouting the curves that would attract members of the opposite sex like bees to honey, he had no idea how to deal with her. He rationalized that this was natural, and would hopefully also pass. She just needed to be around other women, to learn whatever it was they learned while he taught the boy how to do masculine things.

One Friday before Easter, the boy had come home from school with a bloody nose and some abrasions on his face, which after some hard questioning turned out had come about from a fight with an older bully who had been bothering Jasmine during recess; he had grown increasingly abusive and insulting as the day had worn on. The boy had rushed to defend Jasmine's honor, only to be pummeled by the larger student, whose two years of seniority was enhanced by growing up in a household with three brothers who had taught him to fight. The boy's education hadn't yet moved to manual self-defense, but, looking at his bruised face, Emilio decided it was time to teach him how to use his fists.

As with most things, the boy learned quickly and, within a few weeks, had mastered the basics of the primitive form of martial arts Emilio knew; really just a combination of rudimentary boxing and street-fighting techniques. But the boy was a sponge, and once he'd exhausted Emilio's capabilities he lobbied for more advanced training – and given that it was Emilio's job to provide him with the fullest possible education, they researched alternatives and quickly found a plethora of options. Culiacan was the nearest large city, a half hour drive from the ranch. It had a number of martial arts schools specializing in judo, karate, and kung fu. The boy convinced Emilio that his development warranted three classes a week. He added the stylized moves and holds he learned to his exercise routine, striving to perfect those as he had so many others.

There were no more incidents at school after the next altercation – when the boy knocked the older punk unconscious within a few seconds of the fight starting, the bully abruptly lost his taste for hassling Jasmine or picking on either of them. His classmates treated him with polite and cautious deference from that point on.

He didn't mix with the rest of his peers and showed no interest in friendships beyond casual greetings-in-passing in the halls. That was more than enough interaction for him; he viewed his fellow students as inferior in every way – not because he was arrogant, but rather because he'd run an equation and found them wanting and immature. They were children, given to excitement or emotional flights, whereas he was almost an adult, always restrained. He was quiet and withdrawn and tended to keep to himself, preferring to limit his mingling to Jasmine during recess. They had grown close by virtue of their shared male authority figure. It was a brother-sister relationship, for the most part, but the ladies had cautioned both Emilio and Jasmine that things would have to change once they both matured.

Shortly after he turned sixteen and she fifteen the inevitable occurred; the two became inseparable in spite of admonitions from the adults. Jasmine was gorgeous by then, and at an age when many Mexican girls in past generations were married and having their first children, so it was foolish high hope on everyone's part to expect that the two wouldn't find each other, living out in the country as they did, and in the same compound. The boy had grown from a gangly colt into a self-possessed young man with looks that made females glance at him twice, and Jasmine radiated a beauty that was dazzling to behold.

One afternoon after school they had been hanging around the corral, the heat of the approaching summer heavy in the air, and the boy and Jasmine had spied each other across the field and gravitated to the fence, the horses within the enclosure prancing as they trotted around and around, two ranch hands minding them with watchful eyes.

"So, what are you up to?" Jasmine asked, her furtive glance taking in the boy's glistening chest, a thin sheen of perspiration lingering from his afternoon workout.

"Nothing. Same as ever. Last days of school for the year, and constant practice with your father."

"Ah, yes, the practice. That's got to get old after a while," she said, offering a gleaming smile.

"Everything gets old after a while," the boy said, his voice sounding more mature than his years, the timbre having changed that spring from the higher pitch of an adolescent. She took a sidelong glance at him and noticed that he'd begun shaving recently, his upper lip darkened by a dusting of stubble, and something in her lurched at the sight of his chiseled profile.

They watched the horses, and then a third *ranchero* approached leading a large brown stallion, the proud creature tossing its head side to side as it trailed the man. The other two ranchers drove the remaining ponies out of the corral and towards the barn, the way familiar to them from countless days of training, leaving only one tan mare, still frisky with the energy of youth. A fourth cowboy entered the corral, and clicking his tongue, moved to the mare and quieted her, feeding her sugar as he murmured in her ear and stroked her head, her flanks quivering from her earlier exertions.

Jasmine sucked in her breath as the stallion was taken to the mare, and her complexion flushed as the stallion mounted the female and the two horses mated – a not uncommon occurrence on the ranch, but one that had increasingly drawn her interest of late. The boy eyed the proceedings with marginal interest, his attention drawn more by Jasmine's smooth skin and flashing eyes than anything equestrian-related. When the show was over, electricity seemed to crackle between Jasmine and the boy, unspoken but as powerful as a lightning strike.

"Come on. I want to show you something," Jasmine said, her voice tight as she brushed back her glossy black hair with slender fingers, revealing a perfectly sculpted neckline and delicately formed ears, wisps of black curls framing each, small gold studs catching the sun. The boy nodded, swallowing hard, his mouth suddenly dry, and they walked to the edge of the clearing and then into the heavy woods surrounding the ranch.

"Where are you going?" he asked, but she didn't answer with anything but a shush as she led the way.

Eventually they reached a stream they had both spent many summers enjoying, its cool clear water flowed down from the nearby mountains, the rushing of the current over the time-worn rocks musical to their ears. The heat of the day had built to the low-nineties, muggy before an approaching storm, and the change in the atmosphere near the water was palpable.

"I just wanted to get away for a while. It's so damned hot at the house, and there's nothing to do. I'm bored," she complained, her lips flashing the hint of a smile as she took in the stream. "How about you? Don't you get tired, every day the same thing, never anything new? It's driving me crazy..."

He moved to the edge of the bank and picked up a small flat stone, then tossed it into the swirling current.

"Sure. Who wouldn't?" he admitted, and then they both fell silent, contemplating the stream's gentle surge.

Jasmine sat down near the water and then lay back on the grass, considering the configuration of the sparse, puffy clouds overhead as though they held some sort of secret. She shifted her gaze to his face, and when she caught his eye the boy sat next to her, another rock in his hand, his repertoire of small talk exhausted. He'd always been easy in her presence, a familiarity bred from years of proximity, but now, suddenly, everything felt different, and he couldn't think of anything to say. A warm breeze stirred the surrounding trees, and for a moment, time stood still, the perfection of the instant lingering as though it could last forever.

Jasmine rolled towards him and reached up with a trembling hand, then pulled him down to her, no words required. He hesitated for a brief instant and then he was lying next to her, her scent vaguely floral, as inviting as anything he'd ever dreamt of. His lips found hers and his eyes closed even as hers remained open, a faraway look in them neither would have recognized.

The boy's tentative gentleness gradually shifted to a more aggressive confidence, and soon an urgency was building in him that dictated its own pace. Her rhythm matched his, a new, unfamiliar hunger now in control of her, a need that had been little more than a smolder suddenly flaring up to become an out-of-control blaze.

They were both breathless when she pushed him away and sat up, seeming to arrive at an important decision as his awareness returned to the present from whatever miraculous destination he'd found in her arms.

She rose, his puzzled gaze trailing her as she peered at the water, then fixed him with a playful look as she smoothed her dress, her hands lingering on the white cotton a little longer than normal.

"I'm hot. Let's cool off," she said, and then, surprising him as much as anything ever had, Jasmine pulled the light summer dress over her head and kicked off her sandals, her perfect youthful curves clad in only a straining bra and a pair of pink cotton panties. The boy was speechless at the nearly naked immediacy of her nubile body, but before he could regain his composure she had turned from him and slipped her bra off, then taken a tentative step into the water, and then another, the sight of her tan skin and flawless back mesmerizing until she was immersed to her neck in a deep pool ten yards upstream.

"Come on. It's wonderful," she invited, and he glanced down at his shirt and pants, the evidence of his arousal obvious.

He grinned and shrugged, then stripped off his shirt, the hardened slabs of muscle chiseled from his relentless exercise regimen riveting Jasmine's gaze as he stepped out of his shoes, and then he pulled off his jeans and tossed them on top of her dress.

When he made it to Jasmine, in the pool where they had taken their refreshment countless times as children, she welcomed him in a decidedly more mature way, her legs wrapping around his waist as she kissed him again, this time deeper, a low moan escaping from her recesses as their lips and tongues met, and for a fleeting moment he felt like he ruled the world, was capable of anything, a man, now, finally, who had found his elusive meaning in life.

The day passed in a fog of desire, their appetites finally unleashed, the forbidden secrets of each other's bodies now an accessible wonder to be explored. When they returned to the compound three hours later, he first, in order to avoid any suspicion from the staff, followed by Jasmine a short time later, both knew something important had forever changed, and no matter what anyone said, they belonged now, and each answered only to the other, the outside world an annoyance that would never understand what they'd shared.

The couple found time to sneak away even while under near-constant watch, as young lovers often do, confounding the best intentions of their guardians. They'd spend long hours in each other's arms, in the barn, or hidden away in one of the recesses of the main house, or at their original rendezvous spot at the stream. Once they'd fully discovered their passion they were like prisoners who'd crossed a long, dry desert and found themselves at an oasis. Their coupling soon became a daily event and for the first time in his life, the boy found himself enraptured by another human being. His attraction to Jasmine was magnetic and primal, and before long he was hers, body and soul, willing to go to any lengths to be with her or make her happy.

The boy was even willing to entertain Jasmine's quirky ideas about the nature of reality, and indulged her penchant for spirituality and the paranormal, which had gradually developed into a borderline obsession. Every other utterance from her was regarding what fate, or the stars, wanted, which the boy attributed to her exotic nature and bored intellect. But she was deadly serious about her belief that there was more to the universe than what could be proved or seen, and so it was that three months after his sixteenth birthday he found himself agreeing to accompany her to the lair of an old woman who claimed to be a medium, so she could divine his future.

That morning, they set off down the road on their bicycles, followed by a pick-up truck carrying three men wearing cowboy hats and toting assault rifles. Even though *Don* Miguel was hardly ever in evidence, he insisted that the boy be protected at all times as though an attack on the ranch was imminent. This was just another way in which he was different than his cartel brethren – he was a meticulous planner and left nothing to chance. That had stood him in good stead throughout his life; he was ever-vigilant to possible threats to his family or entourage.

When they reached the clapboard hovel where the woman lived and conducted her dubious business, marked with a battered roadside sign ringed with crudely-painted moons and stars proclaiming Madame Sirena to be a medium extraordinaire, the truck pulled to a stop a discreet distance from the dwelling. The young couple leaned their bicycles against the front of the house and, hand-in-hand, ascended the three rickety steps. Jasmine knocked on the door, and flakes of sun-bleached paint dusted her knuckles, the sound of their arrival echoing off the cinderblock walls.

After a considerable pause, the weathered door was opened by an ancient gray-haired woman wearing a red gauze gypsy shawl trimmed in small gold coins. She fixed them both with a one-eyed stare – the vision in her other eye having been lost long ago. The boy felt momentary revulsion when he saw her milky-white pupil, but hid his reaction and braved a tentative smile.

"Ah. So this is the young man! Welcome, Jasmine, *mi amor*. Welcome. Look at him. He's a strapping one, yes? Handsome, you were right about that, and strong as a bull, I'd wager. Come in, come in…," Madame Sirena insisted, gesturing at the gloomy interior with her claw-like hand. The boy noted in passing that she smelled like hastily applied cheap rose water, and sweat – a thoroughly objectionable combination that would stay with him as a reminder of unpleasantness for the rest of his life.

"Here. Sit at the table. Let's see what we have, *eh*? First I'll look at your palm, and see what the gods have written for you in terms of love and life…and then I'll do a reading." She peered at them in the gloom, a crafty expression on her wizened face. "It's customary to leave a tribute for the spirits' divine cooperation in producing an accurate reading, young man," she hissed at him, in what he presumed she imagined to be a sly manner. Jasmine nudged him with her elbow and the boy fumbled in his pocket and fished out a hundred peso note, placing it in the straw bowl the woman had balanced near the table's edge. The bowl and the money quickly disappeared and then the Madame moved around the room, lighting candles and incense. She pushed the button on a portable stereo sitting on a decrepit book shelf; vaguely-Asian music began to drift from the tiny speakers, low volume, atmospheric dissonance to create a mood, more than anything.

The boy studied the walls and noted with amusement that there were countless photographs of mediums and séances and spooky-looking scenes, interspersed with turn-of-the-century posters depicting supernatural events and expositions. The overall effect was somewhat clumsy, but effective for the local peasantry, he supposed. What Jasmine found so fascinating about it all was beyond him, but if it made her happy, so be it. Accepting her fascination without judgment seemed a small enough price to pay to find heaven in her embrace.

The crone approached the table and switched on a dusty yellow hanging lamp with an intricate brocade shade that directed most of the light to the center of the table. She sat across from the boy and gestured at him.

"Give me your hand. The right hand. Palm up. Just relax. This won't hurt. Much," she assured him, then cackled. He wondered whether she'd gotten her act out of central casting for a C-level horror film, the kind that were popular at the local cinemas with badly dubbed Spanish or blurry subtitles. Still, he played along, and dutifully placed his hand on the table.

The woman took it in hers and made a variety of sounds intended to signal deep thought, no doubt.

"Hmmmm. Mmmm...yesssss. Oh. I see your love line is clear. You will only have one real love in your life, and it will be early in your time here. Hmmmm. Your lifeline is different. It's long, but has many breaks, signaling something unusual. Maybe illness, maybe brushes with death. But it continues, so you will prevail through it all...hmmmm."

This went on for a while and he feigned polite interest in the ambiguous generalities about his possible future. Of course, with Jasmine sitting there listening, love *would* be early and intense and genuine, which held an element of truth. When he was with Jasmine, he felt like an eagle soaring above the clouds. The intensity of his feelings for her was almost scary. It gave her power over him, which his training advised him to recoil from. Still, hormones were not to be denied, and he was smitten, that was for sure.

The palm reading finished, the old woman trundled over to a cabinet and withdrew an ancient deck of cards, placing it on the table after shuffling the tattered rectangles for several minutes.

"This is the tarot. It knows all, and tells all. Nobody can hide the truth from the tarot, and its words possess the wisdom of the ages."

Sure they do. A hundred of my pesos' worth, to be exact. Including the cheesy canned tunes and the gypsy act. He wished she'd get on with it. He could think of a dozen different things he'd rather be doing with Jasmine just now, all of them involving nudity and not one of them included an old crone's hackneyed ramblings.

The woman began her ritual, and paused at the end after she'd revealed all the cards. The boy was absently studying the photos on the stained wall behind her, his attention caught by a photograph of a raven, or perhaps a crow, perched on a barbed-wire fence. Something about it chilled his blood, but he didn't know why. He'd tuned out her prattle as his gaze had roamed over the images, thinking thoughts worthy of his energy rather than listening to superstitious mumbo-jumbo.

His awareness grudgingly returned to the table, pulled from the photo of the crow, as the putative Madame contemplated the meaning of the cards. She pointed at several with a trembling finger.

"This is Death. It's placement in the reading is ominous. It can signal many things, but in this sequence, it hints that you will be constantly surrounded by death." The woman continued droning, but the boy was zoning out again. *Gee, good guess.* Living in Culiacan, with *Don* Miguel as your protector and benefactor, you're going to be surrounded by death. What a stretch, and a surprise to one and all. The nonstop weapons and survival training that Jasmine had no doubt chatted with the woman about couldn't have been a tipoff or anything. Hell, all he had to do was close his eyes and he could bring death to the surface, fresh as though it had only occurred just yesterday. Incredibly insightful so far. He was getting his money's worth. What was next? Danger? Uncertainty?

"And this, the defining card, is the King of Swords. But it's inverted. Which is a negative sign. It can mean many things, most of which involve destruction and selfish consequences…"

"Inverted?" the boy asked, finally interested in something she'd said.

"It's upside down," the medium explained in a tremulous voice.

"Not to me," the boy observed. He was sitting opposite her.

They were both correct.

The tense reading drew to an uncomfortable and abrupt close, the woman seeming suddenly anxious to be rid of them. No doubt she felt she'd done enough of her shtick for the hundred pesos and was hoping for more revenue for the day. The boy couldn't believe anyone would buy her laughable song and dance and he was annoyed when Jasmine lingered, murmuring with the old biddy, as they both flicked furtive glances at him.

Once they'd cycled back home, the afternoon sun blazing through the drooping trees that sheltered the road from the worst of the heat, Jasmine had seemed withdrawn and distant, showing no interest in a romantic interlude. She hadn't responded well to the boy's mockery of the reading as they'd pedaled, taking it as a personal affront to her sacred beliefs. In retrospect, he could have chosen his few words with more kindness. 'Baffling bullshit' could be misinterpreted, as could 'superstitious idiocy'.

Whatever the woman's ability to divine the future, one thing changed forever, from that afternoon on. Jasmine and he were never the same, which he directly attributed to the vicious old witch's black predictions. The old crone had the ability to foretell the future, all right, in that she'd initiated a subtle campaign to undermine their relationship, for who knew what reason. But he learned quickly that the power of superstition could be significant – a lesson he would carry forward with him into life. And he vividly remembered the final card that seemed to have such an effect on the venomous old faker – the oldest of the tarot face cards, the reversed King of Swords.

The previous months had passed with the topic of how to deal with the romantic *fait-accompli* aired often among the elders in the compound. It was a constant sticking point between Emilio and the ladies. Emilio was of the opinion that if the boy was going to be sampling his precious hothouse flower's bounty, he should plan on getting married, the sooner the better. The ladies argued against any sort of confrontation, partially because of who he was, as well as mitigating their youth. Neither Jasmine nor the boy had been aware of the seething disagreement their trysts caused, not that either of them would have been particularly interested in the older adults' opinions. The arrogance of youth inevitably believed in its supremacy, and the young were typically convinced that the aged had little grasp of how the modern world worked.

Emilio and the ladies were terrified that the boy would use Jasmine for his pleasure and then break her heart, and so it was with considerable surprise that Emilio found the boy to be increasingly moody and dejected as his sixteenth summer wore on. When Emilio confronted him, the confession that the couple had been intimate came as no shock, but his complaint that Jasmine had become uninterested in him and had decided that they weren't compatible did. Emilio didn't know whether to be angry or relieved, but the boy was suffering, as only those experiencing the tender cuts of young love can, so he redoubled his training and poured on the challenges. The boy lapped it up, growing more adept each day, and eventually moved beyond his infatuation with Jasmine, even as she showed no further appetite for him. It was as though a switch had been thrown – she'd swung from being obviously enamored to wanting nothing to do with him, confounding not only the boy, but also the adults. Still, Emilio sensed that there was unfinished business between the two, and got the impression from the boy that his passage to other girls would be a bitter one, tainted by Jasmine's memory.

From the boy's perspective, Jasmine's rejection was an abandonment, serving to remind him how foolish it was to trust others or allow them into your emotional life. It was during that sixteenth summer that he made the mental resolution to be an island, impenetrable and aloof, using others for his convenience but nothing more. The pain of the only thing he cared about in his life casting him aside was a fork in the road for him, where one possible future had involved love and trust, and the other led down a path where he was alone, suspicious and always on guard. For the first time in his life he'd opened up and entrusted Jasmine with his heart, only to be repaid by her spitting in his face for his trouble. His rigid training provided the solution: never allow anyone to get close, never reveal your true self, and never care.

And so it was that he found a philosophy that was useful, that afforded him some relief in his time of confused pain. Others had no innate value for him beyond what they could do to further his agenda or meet his demands. They were objects that only existed as minor planets orbiting his solar system, in which he was the sun – the giver of life and the destroyer of worlds. His narcissism wasn't unusual for isolated youths who found every task or challenge laughably easy, but the combination of his violent past and Jasmine's snubbing of him, transformed him into the very character that the old medium woman had described when articulating the meaning of the reversed King of Swords – a selfish megalomaniac who would go to any lengths to satisfy his needs, even if it resulted in the destruction of others. The boy had slim interest in considering the ramifications of his chosen worldview. His training now consumed all of his free hours as he sought to exceed even the highest bars Emilio could conjure as challenges. He'd increased his Dojo sessions to five times a week and had quickly mastered most of the offered techniques. His high school had graduated him early due to his advanced academic performance so he set about studying engineering and architecture in earnest, mainly as a guide to understanding how things operated or were built. He had a ravenous intellect unlike any his instructors had ever seen; a young man who could do or be whatever he wanted. The future was beyond bright for him and he soon discovered that there were many willing young females who sought his attention – and so, in time, Jasmine became a distant memory, or so he told himself even as every new conquest brought a reminder of her.

The remainder of his sixteenth year was spent in rigorous pursuit of excellence, whether they were intellectual, physical, or defense-related endeavors. His teen years were a defining period, where he honed his proficiency to a razor's edge. Never before had Emilio seen someone who could shoot as well or expertly disappear into the woods without a sound and become untraceable, or swim as athletically, or remain inscrutable through any circumstance. The discipline Emilio had sought to instill had yielded incredible dividends. The boy was almost superhuman in his commitment and self-possession. It was as though providence had blessed him with a surplus of fitness and acuity. By the time he was due to turn seventeen, Emilio was satisfied that his work with the boy was done. He'd made the transition from boy into young man, and the world was now his playground, to do with as he liked.

Which made it all the more surprising when he vanished without a trace on the morning of his seventeenth birthday, *Don* Miguel dead, and the boy who was like his son gone without a trace.

CHAPTER 4

Eleven years ago, Veracruz, Mexico

The navy base in Veracruz was expansive, crawling with personnel and equipment. This was the primary headquarters for the Gulf region and was where the specialized training for the country's equivalent of the SEALs took place – the *Fuerzas Especiales*, or special forces. This elite team of fighters had just been created after a reorganization of the Navy's marine infantry – the marines. The brass had decided it needed a special response organization that was trained to far higher standards than the already elite marines, and so they formed a group of five hundred specialist commandos, to be trained in explosives, parachuting, military diving, sniping, urban combat and vertical descent. They would be Mexico's ultimate ninja squad, to be used in the most dangerous of circumstances, on the most hazardous of missions.

After the young man had abruptly departed Sinaloa he'd floated around Mexico for a few months, creating the appropriate paperwork so that he could join the navy using a virgin identity. He quickly impressed his commanding officers with his supernatural weapons capabilities and was placed on the fast track for the new group. He was the dream candidate for the job: young, athletic, a prodigy with guns, smart, fearless, and extremely tough. If there had ever been a vocation specially made for him, being one of the new navy commandos was it. Even the motto resonated with him – *Fuerza, Espiritu, Sabiduria*. Force, Spirit and Wisdom. He had all three in abundance and he'd arrived at the perfect place to continue the education he'd begun with Emilio. Much as he'd liked his mentor, it was clear to him that he'd learned all he could and needed to go somewhere designed to produce professionals if he was going to progress as he wanted.

He'd signed up a few months after his seventeenth birthday, although his new paperwork put his age at eighteen and a half. That was a necessary artifice, as was his selection of a name so that he could start anew, without any baggage from his past. The young man was now calling himself Raul Terenova, which was as good as any other, he supposed. Names were unimportant to him. They were disposable, as was most everything in his life.

Raul excelled in the brutal training conditions, which truth be told were kinder and more relaxed than the ones he'd imposed upon himself for years. But he learned a lot, especially on the explosives side. There was nothing like the military to proffer the kind of training you just couldn't get in civilian life, no matter what you did. His goal was to be an expert in every aspect of combat the special forces could teach him, and with his tenacity and discipline, he'd quickly climbed to the top of his class and established records. He became the model for all men who would follow, demanding more from himself than anything his trainers could have mustered. Young Raul was far more motivated than any of his classmates to get all he could out of his service years. He viewed his time with the military as a stepping stone, whereas his peers would go on to be career soldiers.

Becoming a naval commando had been an idea he'd grown fixated with when he was sixteen, after reading about the service's plans to create a group of super soldiers. He didn't have any burning desire to become a marine but if he was going to excel in the field he'd been contemplating, the more skills he had, the more valuable he would be. None of which he told his recruiting officer. To the navy, he'd presented himself as a fiercely patriotic young man who wanted to escape from a dull existence at home in rural Chiapas and don a uniform that would get him instant respect – and a life of adventure and action.

During basic training, he had stood out as far above the quality of the other green recruits. His scores on the written exams had floored the instructors. Here was a candidate who was blisteringly smart, who could swim like a fish, shoot like a marksman, and had the physical prowess of a professional athlete. There had been no question about moving him ahead of the queue and putting him into the specialized marine training – and from there it became obvious that he should be one of the new elite commandos.

Today, they were working on specialized sniping – long range, which was considered to be anything over a thousand meters, or almost thirty-three hundred feet. At such extreme distances, a variety of elements came into play, including wind strength and direction, humidity, temperature, elevation, and rate of movement if it wasn't a stationary target. While there were recorded instances of snipers successfully killing from more than twenty-four hundred meters, those were considered anomalies. At sixteen hundred meters, the target was a mile away. To hit that distance with accuracy was considered virtually impossible for any but an impossibly small group of expert marksmen, although advents like laser rangefinders and computer software that would calculate the various elements had improved the odds.

The day's exercise was on targets at a confirmed distance of a thousand meters, or roughly three quarters of a mile. The rifle they were using for the exercise was an American-manufactured Barrett M82, a .50 caliber rifle with an effective range of eighteen hundred meters, although accuracy became iffy after nine hundred to a thousand meters. Sixteen hundred meters was considered acceptable if you were trying to hit a bomb or something larger than a human torso, but there were too many variables that could affect accuracy. Many snipers preferred the smaller .338 caliber rifles for precision, and the official sniper rifle for the marines was the Heckler & Koch PSG1 firing a 7.65 millimeter round. The problem was that the weapon's accuracy dropped off at eight hundred meters, so special forces had secured fifteen of the much larger payload Barrett rifles as a trial for standardization – a substitute for the smaller PSG1.

Each sniper cadet had been assigned a coach, who gave the firing order and then received a report from down-field. Accuracy had dropped off markedly once the seven hundred meter threshold had been crossed, and there were few who could deliver precise hits at over eight hundred.

"What does your nose tell you?" the coach asked Raul.

"Moderate humidity."

"Guesstimate on wind speed and direction?"

"Seven to ten knots, out of the north-east," Raul replied.

"Temperature?"

"Thirty degrees Celsius."

"We're going to do this without the computer. Purely based on your observations. If you're confident in your observations, adjust your bearings accordingly. Good luck," the coach said, and then stepped back, leaving the young man to himself.

Raul concentrated on controlling his breathing, and soon his entire awareness was synthesized into the tiny world within the scope. He made some minor corrections for his wind-speed guesstimate then gently massaged the trigger until the weapon fired, slamming into his shoulder with its considerable recoil. He'd long ago learned never to pull the trigger, as it could throw off accuracy. A deliberate squeeze was best.

The radio crackled and the report came back. A bull's-eye.

"Good shooting."

They repeated the exercise for ten shots, all of which landed within a ten inch grouping.

"I think we're done here, young man."

Raul looked up at the coach. He was emboldened by his success, and wanted to try for a personal best. He got along well with the man, so he floated his idea.

"Why don't we try it at fifteen-hundred meters? Just to make it interesting?" Raul suggested.

The coach looked at him like he was crazy. "Pretty cocky, huh? That's an impossible range with that weapon and that ammo, not to mention that scope. You want to put money on it?" the coach asked. Fifteen hundred meters was just under a mile away, and was near the absolute maximum of the rifle's range for a human-sized target.

"Two hundred pesos says I nail it three out of five. Although I agree that this ammo is crap for that distance. I'd prefer to load it myself for better consistency, but hey...," Raul said.

"Fine. But three misses, we go home and I'm two hundred richer."

The coach got on the radio and issued the instructions to the man downrange, who obligingly moved the target to the farthest point on the field before taking cover.

"It's your funeral. Fire when ready," the coach said.

Raul took his time, made further adjustments to the scope, then repeated his meditation process where he became one with the weapon. The discharge almost startled him, so focused was his concentration. There was no need to wait for the radio to report. He knew what it would say.

"Bull's-eye, twenty centimeters off center," the radio crackled.

"To the right, or the left? Or low or high? Tell him to be specific, would you?" Raul groused.

Wide-eyed, the coach studied Raul like he was from another planet, then posed the question.

The response came back. "To the right."

"That's what I thought he'd say. Wind's died down a hair in the last thirty seconds. Tell him to clear," Raul said.

Once he got the go ahead, he repeated the impossible shot. Four more times. All shots grouped with under a foot of variance.

The coach gladly handed over the two hundred pesos for the single most astounding display of marksmanship he'd ever witnessed.

"You're a fucking monster, you know that? That's superhuman voodoo shit right there. I've never seen anything like it, and I've been teaching for over ten years. Before that, I was one of the top three marksmen in Mexico," the coach acceded, studying him with a kind of wonder.

"Those that can, do…"

Both men laughed together, in spite of a twenty-five-year age difference. Raul would never again shoot with that accuracy at that distance, preferring to limit his performance to more average expectations. It wouldn't do to show off, or to develop too much of a reputation. Better to have had a one in a million day and then graduate in the top third of the class than at the top. He remembered Emilio's sage counsel from when he was just a sprout. Never show too much of your hand. To give your enemies information is to make a gift. And friends can become enemies. So know how good you are and then take private pleasure in that accomplishment. Becoming celebrated makes you a target. Better to be in the middle of the herd when the hunters come than at the head.

Into the evening, Raul enjoyed his place in the spotlight amongst his peers, as news of his exploit circulated. As much as he enjoyed the adulation, a part of him knew that the hubris that came from being the best was a fickle charm, so he resolved to enjoy it for now, because it would be the last time he allowed others to get a glimpse of what he could actually do. Information was power, and allowing, no, *inviting* others to understand his capabilities was foolhardy.

His goal was to drain what experience he could from the service and then slip away like a ghost. It would serve no useful purpose to be noticed any more than he already had been. From that point on he would adopt a lower profile and continue to accumulate the pearls of experience until his work there was done. He calculated that another three months of training and perhaps six months in the field would be sufficient, making for a total of a year and a half of his life devoted to the pursuit of excellence with Mexico's finest.

That night, as he lay his head upon his bunk, he began a silent mental countdown.

To when he could begin his new, new life.

Patience, he told himself, was a virtue that would pay enormous dividends – it became his bedtime mantra. He needed to maximize his learning while he was still in school. That's how he viewed his life to the point he'd arrived at – it was his education. The time would soon come when the pupil proved himself to be the master, but for now, he had lessons to absorb. He still wanted to learn special operations parachuting – not jumping out of planes and controlling his descent, but rather precision-guiding his drop to within a meter of his target point, from both high-altitude and low, which required different skills. And he still needed more hours of scuba time, as well as some orientation on flying planes and helicopters. The latter two weren't on the curriculum, but he was lobbying to get them added. You could never know too much.

With visions of his future cascading through his awareness, he slowly drifted off to sleep, his day's toil finally at an end.

CHAPTER 5

Ten and a half years ago, Veracruz, Mexico

The battered, rusting hull of the freighter ground against the old tires fastened to the concrete dock at one of the more remote cargo offloading piers on Veracruz harbor. Flying a Panamanian flag, *Caruso* was at least forty years old, and had made the long trip from South America countless times. The dark green paint on her dented steel sides bubbled at the rivets from underlying rust. She looked to be on her last legs, as did many of the freighters that made their way into the busy deep water port. The old ship was manifested as delivering coffee and bananas from Colombia, which was largely true, although the money-making haul was the ten tons of cocaine stashed in the specially constructed compartments in her lower hold, which to cursory inspection appeared to be the floor of the cargo area inside the hull. Even if a nosy customs inspector had cared to pry open one of the scarred hatches, all he would have found was what appeared to be the slimy metal lining of the waterlogged bilge. It was an ingenious design; the modifications had taken place at a discreet shipyard in Colon, Panama while other refits were being attended to.

A veteran of the ongoing, frequent trade between South America and Mexico, *Caruso* was just one of thousands of vessels that offloaded cargo each year in Veracruz, the principal importation hub for Eastern Mexico. Under normal circumstances she would have rendezvoused with a commercial fishing boat out in the Gulf of Mexico to transfer her illicit wares, well away from prying eyes, but the shrimper that had been the scheduled drop-off had experienced engine problems eighty miles en-route, so the hook-up had been cancelled. That had left the captain with two choices – toss ten tons of cocaine overboard and lose the shipment and his tidy slice of the profits, or hope that the receiving group could arrange for an alternative offloading plan while the ship was laid over in Veracruz for two days. Worst case, she could steam out, supposedly empty, on her way back to Colombia for more fruit and java, and meet with another boat; but every minute *Caruso* sat in the harbor she was in jeopardy.

Particularly tonight, when *La Familia*, a rival splinter faction of the Gulf cartel, had decided to use the Mexican marines as a vehicle to cause their competitors grief, by tipping law enforcement off to the shipment. It was not unusual for the cartels to exchange information with the military or the police to create problems for their enemies – most of the drug seizures that took place did so because of the constant infighting and jockeying for advantage that was a routine aspect of the trade. It was far more ergonomic to use the military's muscle instead of your own, and if the rivals got into a firefight in the process, so much the better.

The marines had long been considered the only incorruptible branch of the military. The army was notoriously riddled with rot but the marines, for whatever reason, couldn't be bought off, and so were the most feared of the law enforcement branches. In Mexico, the army and navy worked alongside the police and *Federales* for internal security, which included battling the drug cartels, especially since the recent reorganization into more specialized groups. It hadn't been broadly publicized, but since 2000, when Vincente Fox became president of Mexico, the country had been embroiled in a de facto civil war, with the cartels having far greater resources than the army and navy. The total budget for the army was less than a percent of GDP, which put it at considerably under a billion dollars. Contrast that to the over fifty billion dollars per year in wholesale value of cocaine that moved through the cartels. At an eighty to ninety percent margin, that left the *narcotraficantes* with vastly greater resources than the army.

Since the Mexicans had taken over cocaine trafficking for the Colombians, and begun manufacturing methamphetamines in earnest, the money had gotten crazy. Mexico found itself in much the same situation Colombia had faced in the 1980s and 1990s, when it was routine for judges, police chiefs and army generals to be executed en masse by the Colombian cartels, or rather their armed enforcers; the myriad purportedly revolutionary groups that controlled half the country and increasingly acted as private armies for the drug lords.

The lion's share of the profits had shifted from Colombia to Mexico as Colombia contented itself with the far lower-risk and less violent business of production, leaving the transport and distribution to their better-positioned Mexican associates. The profits in Colombia were still significant, with one to two hundred percent markup to the Mexicans, but the margin in trafficking internationally was five to tenfold. A kilo of cocaine that cost the Mexicans twenty-five hundred to three-thousand dollars in Colombia would fetch twenty-five thousand a kilo wholesale across the U.S. border, and that was usually significantly cut with buffering agents in order to dilute the nearly pure cocaine, thereby increasing the apparent quantity once repackaged for the States; so in actuality it was more like an effective thirty to thirty-five thousand sale price for that original kilo by the end of the day.

The incredible margins were a direct function of the illegality of the substances in the target market – the United States. As with alcohol margins during the ill-fated experiment of Prohibition in the 1930s, criminalization of drugs turned what would have been a five percent profit business into a thousand or more percent trade, which created windfall profits for everyone in the supply chain and also created a situation where every aspect was worth killing for. There were no open gun battles over cigarette or alcohol profits because once a substance was legal, the efficiencies of the distribution chains kicked in and it became a boring commercial enterprise. But keeping the substances illegal, especially since they were in huge demand, caused profits to go through the roof.

And so it was that a group of provincial, unsophisticated Mexican farmers became the most powerful narcotics trafficking empires in the world, commanding the sorts of budgets that were the envy of many medium-sized countries. Mexico bore the brunt of the violence that ensued from the power struggles, principally because it was the geographic gateway to the largest market for drugs in the world – the United States.

The harbor was quiet at three a.m., and the wharf area where *Caruso* was tethered was deserted, save for two men smoking cigarettes on the concrete pier, and an uninterested security guard at the massive dock's entry point, where it connected to land. The marines had taken position in the surrounding buildings, having been told that there was a complement of at least a dozen heavily armed men on board, guarding against any incursions to steal their precious cargo.

The leader of the commando team made a series of hand signals, and the men fanned out, while Raul set up his rifle tripod and adjusted his scope. Range was six hundred meters at the closest point, which would be a cakewalk for him were it not for the twenty knot gusting breeze he'd need to factor in. This was his first active operation since graduating from the special forces course so he felt a tingle of anticipation before finally testing his skills in a real-world environment. Shooting at paper targets or silhouettes on a range was one thing, but being in the thick of it with enemies who were shooting back was quite another.

This operation would be a tricky one, in that the commander didn't want to get into a gun battle if he didn't have to. His first plan was to use subterfuge and approach the vessel with several plain-clothed men under his command, subdue the two lookouts with stun guns, and then move the bulk of the commandos swiftly down the dock to the gangplank, boarding the old scow before anyone knew what had happened. Raul had questioned the logic involved but didn't say anything. If it had been his operation he would have approached with a half dozen well-armed divers from the waterside, and used lines to climb up the side of the ship, or alternatively, taken out the two smoking sentries from the harbor end of the dock, firing from the waterline and killing them instantly before moving his squad onto the pier from the water, where nobody would be expecting any attack.

If he was one of the smugglers on the ship, and the marines' intelligence on the number of armed men was correct, he would have had at least two lookouts, one with a night-vision scope, surveying the dock for the slightest hint of trouble. If there was going to be a gun battle, you'd want to pick the distance at which you engaged wisely, in order to be able to hold off any assailants while you made an escape. He'd have had a high-speed tender secured to the ship's stern as a get-away contingency, and would also have had a man watching the water approach, just in case. Because you never, ever really knew – you had to expect the unexpected.

But it wasn't his place to second-guess his superiors and he was interested to see how the exercise would play out. He gave the marines a less than twenty percent chance of taking the ship without a battle, which meant that he'd see some real action. Finally. Albeit from a distance but, in truth, that was preferred. He'd long ago concluded that it was far safer to be sniping from afar than to be a hero rushing into a hail of slugs. Leave that to his peers. He'd pick off his targets with surgical precision before they knew what hit them.

Two large Norwegian wharf rats scurried down the dock, away from the ship and the two smoking men.

These were big rodents; their bodies were a good eighteen inches long, with tails to match – scavengers the size of small dogs. The pier area was infested with them and the city had long ago given up on trying to bring the population under control. Poison had been only moderately effective, and one genius had the idea of releasing a horde of hungry felines – which had resulted in a feral cat infestation in addition to the rats, which were large enough to go ten rounds with a cat without breaking a sweat. Slicks of oil floated on the surface of the water from leaking bilges; the port had a pervasive odor of decay and long-dead fish, and the particular petroleum stink common to industrial waterfronts the world over.

Raul studied the battered ship's bridge for signs of life, scanning slowly over the superstructure and taking his time at each of the helm's reinforced windows. Those would pose a problem, as they'd be at least inch-thick glass, designed to withstand the pressure of the massive waves that could surge over the four hundred feet of bow and ship and slam into the tower. He knew from his reading that oceangoing vessels were designed to withstand seas up to sixty feet in height, the theory being that waves didn't get any larger than that. Of course, the hundred foot rogue waves that had been recorded with some regularity were ignored by the industry because if you built ships that could survive those, they would be too expensive. So everyone pretended that sixty was the maximum, and when hundreds of boats were lost in any given period, it was shoulder shrugs and profit statements that everyone focused on.

His night-vision scope illuminated the bridge in an eerie green. There were two armed sentries visible on the superstructure, one outside on the bridge walkway, and the other inside. He could just make out the gleam of binoculars from the interior, so in Raul's opinion the chances of the commander's scheme working had diminished to less than zero. He was glad it wasn't his ass on the line for this one.

Perhaps, instead of the sea approach, Raul might have had a flight of four to six men parachute in, touching down on the rear of the ship, taking out the sentries as they descended. Virtually anything other than a direct assault down the dock. No wonder the military casualties in the drug wars were so high. With operational plans that amounted to brandishing a saber and screaming, 'Charge!' there could be little expectation of anything but a blood bath. He didn't envy his fellow commandos their duty tonight. There was no way this would go well.

He adjusted his scope to compensate for the stiffening wind, and calculate the distance with his laser rangefinder. Six-hundred seventy-four meters. Like shooting fish in a barrel, he thought, allowing himself the private luxury of a small smile. His face, like those of his fellow commandos, was blacked out with camouflage paint so as to avoid giving off any shine, lending his profile an evil glint akin to that of an escaped demon. The smile was anything but reassuring.

The commander gave the signal and the two undercover men exited the building, one holding a bottle of mescal in his hand and talking loudly in an inebriated slur. Given that there was no way they wouldn't be spotted, the bright idea was that they were to be friendly, drunken dock workers, and once the two smoking guards were dispatched, they would pretend to engage in a scuffle and some 'security guards' would come running to break up the fight. When there were six men in total by the gangplank they'd breach the ship, and more would pour out of the building and reinforce them from there. In addition to the stun guns, the men on the dock would be equipped with grenades and machine pistols, as would the bogus security guards, so the presumption was that they could take the ship by surprise and keep the foe engaged until the main body of commandos made it down the dock. They had two vehicles waiting to race out, filled with armed men who could be at the gangplank in fifteen seconds from the time the signal was given. It seemed like suicide to Raul, but it wasn't his job to craft a better plan. He was only there to shoot, which he was now perfectly positioned to do.

This may have been his first assault but he had enough common sense to understand that even when the commandos prevailed, and they would prevail eventually due to vastly larger numbers, the cost in human life would be high on both sides, whereas a surgical strike could have accomplished much the same result with minimal special forces casualties. It was inefficient, which offended his sense of symmetry more than anything.

He watched as the two men staggered their way down the pier and then returned his full attention to the bridge. The pair of undercover operatives, by the time they made it to the two sentries, would be out of sight of the bridge due to the angle of the hull. Unless of course, the two guards moved, in which case the plan would be a disaster, or alternatively, would need to be aborted. Walking headfirst into a killing zone was generally bad strategy anywhere in the world, not just in Mexico, and he couldn't see the commander barreling forward if the plan was doomed to failure. At least he hoped not.

The sentry on the exterior of the bridge was carrying a machine pistol of some sort – it looked like an Uzi to Raul. That meant limited useful range and accuracy. The Uzi was an antiquated design with an effective range of two hundred meters, which was fine for typical close-quarter urban combat, but lousy for applications requiring accuracy at a distance. A better and more popular choice as far as Raul was concerned was the Kalashnikov AKM, the modernized version of the venerated AK-47, which had double the effective range in single fire mode, or at least three hundred meters when fired full-auto; or probably the best weapon, and his personal favorite for dependability and accuracy in a mid-range assault rifle, the American-built M4. Its five-hundred-meter effective range and extremely high muzzle velocity made it the ideal choice for assault applications, which more than compensated for its relatively small slug size. He'd fired all three with Emilio for years and could disassemble and reassemble any of them in a matter of seconds, so he knew whereof he spoke.

Their luck wasn't going well so far. The two smoking sentries on the dock moved toward the men, so any engagement would take place in plain sight of the bridge. That would mean a full-blown firefight with no cover, likely with a very high toll on the special forces' side. He exhaled, stilling his mind in preparation for the imminent attack, and zeroed the Barrett M82 sniper rifle in on the bridge sentry's upper torso. The .50 caliber M1022 slug would tear a hole through him the size of a baseball at that range so there was no question in his mind that it would only take a single trigger pull to dispatch him. It would be a few more seconds before the shit hit the fan so he slid two more full magazines next to the rifle, where he could quickly change them out once he was empty. The man in the bridge was still his biggest concern. He made a mental note to always carry one magazine of full-jacketed armor-piercing rounds in case he needed to slice through an inch of metal or reinforced glass.

It was show time. He fixed the bridge target in the crosshairs and waited for instruction. The commander was watching the approach and not liking what he saw. He, like Raul, understood that if the bridge sentries weren't caught unawares, the assault would become a slaughterhouse, with his men taking heavy casualties. After struggling with an internal debate, the commander murmured into the com system. One of the two men on the dock had an earpiece, and upon hearing the commander's instructions, grabbed his friend and turned him around, as if only now noticing the two smoking men cautiously approaching them. The mission had been aborted.

"Shit," the commander hissed, and began pacing, mulling over his choices. Now they'd probably have to just pull up in armored vehicles and do this the hard way, shooting it out with no element of surprise.

Raul bit his tongue, but then decided to advance his idea, purely in the interests of keeping his role in the assault interesting and getting some more practical experience. Taking out a single sentry from almost a thousand meters wasn't really much of a challenge. It was a single shot. Maybe two, if they would send someone to find some armor-piercing rounds.

"Sir. Might I have a word?" Raul asked.

The commander regarded him with surprise. Raul was one of his best men, but he never spoke. He was a loner, with no close relationships within the corps.

"This isn't a great moment."

"Yes, sir. I know, sir. I just had an observation that came to me as I was watching the target that may be of some use to you, sir," Raul explained, sucking up his pride and taking the expected supplicant tone.

"Very well. Make it quick," the commander barked. "We need to coordinate a frontal assault before this goes on much longer."

"Permission to approach, sir?"

"Get on with it."

Raul moved to the commander's side, and spoke in a low, calm tone, explaining his ideas and arguing for an amphibian assault. The commander listened carefully, and then cut him off after forty-five seconds.

"That would require far more stealth and luck than we've had tonight. It's a good strategy, and I appreciate your sharing it with me, but I don't think we can afford to waste two more hours preparing it. No, I think we'll do a good old-fashioned frontal assault and take our punches. In the end, we'd have to do one anyway if your plan failed, so my call is to just cut to the chase," the commander declared, summarily dismissing the idea.

Raul considered arguing the point and then decided that he didn't care that much. He'd still get to shoot a couple of bad guys, at least, and what did he care in the end if half the squad got mowed down?

"Yes, sir. Thank you for hearing me out, sir. If we're going to do a frontal, could I please get a magazine of armor-piercing rounds? They'll come in handy to take out the gunman inside the bridge," Raul requested.

The commander nodded and called on the com to one of the team members waiting in the next building.

"Twenty minutes. You'll have 'em. We'll move in thirty."

The commander spun around and began issuing orders in preparation for a brute-force assault. They'd need a couple of armored personnel carriers – enough to carry forty men. He ordered up two Unimog armored trucks and two BTR-70 armored carriers: eight-wheeled vehicles that could accommodate seven commandos each, along with a three man crew to operate the turret-mounted 14.5 mm heavy machine gun and smaller 7.62 mm machine gun. The fallback plan was much more straightforward. Drive up to the ship. Deploy men if no firing takes place and seize the ship. If the sentries or crew decided to shoot it out, blast away at everything in sight and shoot their way through the ship until the crew either surrendered, or was dead. It was inelegant and would result in a lot of bullets flying but it had the benefit of simplicity.

Twenty-five minutes later, a young commando approached Raul and handed him a magazine with five rounds of armor-piercing .50 caliber bullets, apologizing that they couldn't find any more at such short notice. Raul thanked him, and emptied half of one of the spare magazines, counting out five shells and replacing them with the five armor-piercing rounds. He ejected the current bullet in the rifle and chambered one of the new armor-piercing cartridges, then returned to watching the sentries through his night-vision scope.

The commander checked his watch, and at precisely three-forty a.m. ordered the assault, after which everything happened quickly. The two gray BTR-70s, which resembled small tanks more than anything else, rumbled around the corner and out onto the pier, followed by the two hulking trucks. The sentries on the dock froze, staring in numb disbelief at the apparition, and then hurriedly scuttled up the gangplank and disappeared up into the ship. One man's head reappeared for a few seconds and then the gangplank collapsed onto the concrete pier below. The crash was almost immediately followed by the steel watertight door slamming shut with a boom. As it was barred from within, the grinding of the cogs was audible halfway down the dock, even over the baritone growl of the vehicles.

It was going to be considerably harder to take the freighter now because the traffickers were forewarned. The easy access to the ship from the gangplank was gone and the commandos on the dock would be in a siege situation against a ship whose hull rose easily four stories above the pier, with no obvious entry point available. The commander watched in a kind of frozen frustration, and then the shooting started; gunmen emerged from the interior of the ship, moved to the edge of the hull and began firing from behind the protection of the heavy steel from which the hardy old vessel was built.

Raul took in the situation for a few moments, waiting for the right instant, and squeezed the trigger. The gun's boom was deafening. Ears ringing, he watched with satisfaction as both the sentry standing outside the bridge and the man inside collapsed. He'd timed it so that he fired when the outside man was directly in front of the man inside the bridge, effectively killing two birds with one armor-piercing stone. No reason to waste his precious ammo, after all.

He swiveled his attention to the hull, where he could just make out heads popping up here and there, like a nocturnal version of whack-a-mole at a fairground stall. A man wearing a baseball cap leaned over the railing and fired his weapon at the vehicles below. Raul caressed the trigger again and watched as the shooter's head vaporized. Moving down the line, he waited for an opening and took out another. He was now four down with three shells, which he felt was a fair contribution to the ensuing train wreck of an operation. Raul peered through the scope, trying to find any other obvious targets, but the gunmen along the side of the ship had figured out there was a sniper at work, and had retreated into the superstructure, barring the watertight deck entry door in the process.

The gun turrets on the BTR-70s opened up with their armor-piercing rounds, but quickly discovered that their shells, which could easily penetrate up to a one and a half inch steel plate, were just denting the massive hull, which had been fashioned from considerably thicker material. That left the commandos and the traffickers in a classic Mexican standoff. Shooting from the ship had stopped other than from a lone gunman who hadn't made it inside in time, but was behind the bulk of the bridge's tower and so out of Raul's line of sight. Firing from the two BTR-70s had also stopped, though the entire waterfront area still resonated with receding echoes of gunfire.

The commander barked orders into the radio and the men emptied from the personnel carriers and took up position to mount an assault. The men below flung three grappling hooks affixed to black nylon rope over the hull's edge. The four-pronged hooks all found a purchase. The problem was that any men on the ropes who got caught in the fire from the remaining gunman were dead meat, so nobody wanted to be the first to climb four stories up onto the deck. Raul decided to shift his position and moved down the row of warehouse windows until he was more symmetrically placed and could see down the entire length of the ship.

He set his rifle tripod down, careful not to jar the weapon, and resumed peering through the scope. There, at the farthest end of the ship, right near the stern, was the gunman, taking cover below the three-foot-high lip of the boat's deck edge. Raul calculated the distance and added an additional forty yards and adjusted accordingly, then waited for the man's head to pop back up. It was just a matter of time, he figured – correctly, as it turned out – and his vigilance was rewarded by the man's arms and head coming into view as he prepared to empty his weapon at the commandos below. Raul took his shot, and the man's head dissolved in a bloody spray of fragments.

The deck was now empty, although it would still be ugly fighting through the ship. Not his problem.

The commander gave the squad the all-clear signal, and within seconds commandos were moving swiftly up the ropes to the ship above. Raul had shifted his attention to the bridge windows again, figuring it would just be a matter of time until some bright lad figured out that he could shoot from the portholes that stretched another four stories above the ship's deck, picking off soldiers as they climbed over the rail. Sure enough, one of the glass hatches on the side opened, and a gun barrel poked out.

He waited patiently because the angle of the shooter's barrel wouldn't allow him to hit the deck, and sure enough, more of the weapon slowly emerged from the window until Raul also saw the arm that was holding it. The first commandos were only a few feet from the edge so he only had a second before they'd be exposed to the gunman. Raul fired, and the assault rifle tumbled harmlessly to the deck below, taking three quarters of the man's still-attached arm with it.

That would give the rest inside something to think about.

From there on out it was a textbook incursion. They had to use explosives to blow the doors open, and for fifteen minutes, bursts of gunfire echoed throughout the boat's hull. Eventually the commander got an all clear call from the men inside, and a status report. They'd taken out six hostiles, no survivors, and lost nine men in the process. Raul listened to the recitation impassively, his face betraying nothing. The commander glanced at him as he heard the casualty assessment, but Raul was busy packing up his gear, his work for the night finished. The commander approached him and stopped a few feet away, studying the silent sniper as he finished stowing his weapon into a long padded case.

"Great shooting. You saved a lot of lives tonight," the commander said.

Raul bit his tongue, didn't blurt out his natural reaction, which was that if he'd been allowed to lead an amphibian team they would have likely lost only a few men, if any, thanks to the element of surprise, and that the commander had killed those commandos with his lack of flair and imagination just as surely as if he'd pulled the trigger himself. Instead, he nodded and stood, shouldering the rifle case and hoisting his bag.

"Thank you, sir. I had some lucky shots tonight. We were all fortunate."

There being nothing more to say, he saluted with his free hand before descending the stairs to join the remainder of his team. It would be a long stretch of duty as the bodies were recovered and the drugs inventoried and he wanted to get out of the commander's sight before his contempt for the man leaked through his veneer. It wasn't worth it. Most of the world was composed of idiots – the commander was simply one dolt of many, and nothing Raul said or did would change things.

It was that night, on his first live operation, that he realized he'd probably already learned everything he was going to from the military. The time had already come, after little over a year in the service, to reconsider his options.

CHAPTER 6

Ten years ago, Sinaloa, Mexico

Eighteen months after joining the marines, Raul disappeared without a trace, leaving nothing behind to be remembered by except his assumed name, which he'd quickly grown to despise. He'd participated in seven more operations after his first one, and with each mission he became more convinced that his talents were being wasted and he wasn't progressing any further. To make matters worse, he witnessed countless acts of bumbling bureaucracy by the ranking officers, costing the men under their command casualties for no good reason. If anything had ever convinced him that he wouldn't do well working for someone else, his half year of active duty after completing his boot camp and all the specialized training had done the trick. When he walked off the base for the last time, ostensibly on two day's leave to go visit his fictional family in Chiapas, it was with an audible sigh of relief.

Raul had saved almost all of his meager pay and still had a few thousand dollars from the money he'd left home with, after selling his weapons to convert his assets into cash. His identity papers had cost him six hundred dollars in Mexico City, and he'd done some odd jobs before joining the navy, but he would need to put the next part of his grand plan into operation fairly soon if he was going to avoid having to work as a day laborer. Fortunately, the cartels he'd been battling were generous employers, able to pay far more than the navy, so he could pretty much choose which cartel he wanted to approach; as an ex-marine they'd be eager to have him as part of their enforcement team. Although he had different ideas about how he could be of service to them.

He was now three months shy of his nineteenth birthday and free to do as he pleased. Yet there was some unfinished business he needed to attend to back in Sinaloa before he moved on to the next phase of his life. His departure had stuck in his craw, and he felt a pull to return – while he'd told himself that he was completely over Jasmine, the truth was that a part of him had always assumed that her rejection had been some sort of youthful power play, and that she'd get over it and see reason in time. Whether or not that was deluded wishful thinking, he needed to put it behind him once and for all, and with time on his hands and a more mature perspective, he decided to return to his old haunts and see for himself how things now sat. He'd learned to trust his judgment on these things, so he hopped on a bus and began the long trip from Veracruz to Culiacan. Wearing the uniform of a special forces commando, he was afforded privilege by the bus company so thankfully it cost him almost nothing to cross the nation. Two days after he'd left his naval career behind, he descended the stairs in Culiacan, blinking into the bright sunlight of an early spring day.

After forty-two hours cramped on buses, eating whatever junk he could get at the irregular stops, his first order of business was to have a decent meal. He set off in search of a restaurant that had been his favorite, back in the day. Outside the terminal, he hailed a cab, reciting the address from memory to the driver as he slid into the back seat. The young man had changed since he'd last been in town, as had the city itself, growing by leaps and bounds. His carefully trimmed goatee and closely cropped military haircut ensured nobody would recognize him, which wasn't much of an issue considering his long absence. He'd developed into a hardened combat veteran since leaving as a teen boy and his bearing and additional muscle weight filled out his uniform, lending him a formidable presence. The boy had left and had returned a man.

The taxi arrived at the restaurant, *La Chuparrosa Enamorada*, nestled on the banks of the *Canal Rosales*. The young man paid the driver and stepped out onto the pavement, hoisting his duffle as he studied the restaurant façade. It was a Tuesday, so the breakfast business was thin, which wouldn't have been the case had it been the weekend. The place typically had a standing-room crowd on Saturdays and Sundays, due to the generous portions of mouthwatering food and the soothing waterside ambiance. He had been there a few times with Emilio on special occasions and it was one of the things that had been on his mind since boarding the bus in Veracruz. When he entered the large dining room, his boots thumping on the saltillo tile floor, the waitress approached and invited him to an outdoor table overlooking the water. After a cursory glance at the familiar menu, he ordered a glass of orange juice and a plate of chicken *chilaquiles* in red sauce – a local favorite and one of the restaurant's signature dishes.

While he waited for his food to come he thought about his next move, glancing around absently as he remarked to himself on how little things had changed there in the last twenty months. In this sleepy area, things seemed to always remain the same, even as the city grew at an unprecedented rate. The waitress arrived with a heaping platter of breakfast, and as he tucked in he ran down his mental list. The first thing he would need to do was secure reliable transportation. Taxis weren't going to be an option for what he had in mind, so he'd need to get some sort of conveyance sooner rather than later. With his bankroll being as thin as it was, that meant stealing something, or probably several somethings, depending on how far he decided to travel.

He munched on his food, savoring the rich, spicy sauce, and cleaned his plate as efficiently as a dishwasher would. Stuffed, he paid the bill and strolled out onto the rural road, scanning the surroundings for something he could liberate opportunistically. It took him half an hour to spot a suitable vehicle that was easy enough to break into and hotwire, but he eventually found a thirty-year-old Chevrolet truck with a broken wind wing. Within seconds, he was in the cab, scanning the surrounding street to ensure that he hadn't been detected. It took him ten seconds to find the ignition wires and soon he was meandering down the familiar road that led to *Don* Miguel's estate. The landscape was still verdant and wild, nature seemingly impatient to encroach on the slim progress man had introduced. When he was a quarter mile from the turnoff to the ranch, he pulled the old truck onto a dirt track that led into the wilds and parked where it couldn't be seen from the road. He had no idea what he would find at the hacienda when he made it to the estate, but he'd learned to be cautious about everything and considered it best to err on the side of prudence.

He moved stealthily through the woods until he found one of the myriad game trails that ran through the immense tract of *Don* Miguel's property, and soon was jogging along as he had in the old days. It was cool in February so he barely broke a sweat as he moved effortlessly through the foliage. Before long, he was in the cluster of trees that ran along the side of the property, near the horse barn where he'd so long ago been set to move hay as the commencement of his training. He paused momentarily, ears straining for any hint of habitation, but he detected nothing. The main house was deserted, with none of the security men that were everywhere when he'd been living there. No matter; he hadn't come for anything in the house. He wanted to see his mentor, Emilio, and of course, his daughter. For all his efforts Jasmine had survived in the place she'd carved out of his psyche, and he wanted to bring closure to a door that bulged, and threatened to burst open in his recurring dreams.

The young man continued along the perimeter and down the track until he reached the caretaker's house that reposed several hundred yards into the woods. He knew that trail like he'd been on it only yesterday, the loosely placed flagstone that served as a driveway all too familiar under his feet. Surprisingly, he felt a buzz of anxiety in the pit of his stomach as he neared the front door – an altogether alien sensation for him. There, sitting as it always had, was the modest colonial home, deliberately styled in a rustic, sponge-painted manner to mirror the design sensibility of the larger main house, but absent the more flamboyant frills.

Pausing on the front porch, he registered that there was something different about the home than the last time he'd seen it, almost two years ago. It seemed quiet, as though nobody was living there – much like the main estate had appeared from a distance. Shaking off the sense of foreboding, he knocked on the door, and when he heard nothing from inside, he walked around the side to where Emilio parked his big navy blue Ford Lobo crew-cab truck. There it sat, unchanged, next to the small Chevy econo-box Emilio had bought for Jasmine with his bonuses from *Don* Miguel.

He moved back onto the porch, and knocked again.

"Emilio. Jasmine. Please. Open the door. It's me…I'm back…" he yelled.

From inside, he heard a faint rustling, and then Jasmine's distinctive voice.

"Go away. There's nothing for you here."

"Jasmine. Please. Open the door. I need to talk to your father. It's important," he tried again.

"He's dead. Everyone's dead. *Don* Miguel, my father, his sister and his mother. There's only me left now, and I don't want to see you. Please. Just leave. Go now, and stay away," Jasmine warned.

"Dead? How? How is that possible? What's happened since I left? Tell me, Jasmine. Please. Just open the door. I don't want to have this conversation through a slab of wood. I just travelled over a thousand miles to see you…please, Jasmine. I'm begging you. I need to see you."

"No you don't. You left without a word to anyone, and now death has come to the valley, and it's only me left alive – and you. Do yourself a favor, and leave now, while you can," Jasmine implored him.

"If you don't open the door, I'll break in. You know I can find a way. Jasmine, please. This has gone on long enough. Open the damned door so we can speak like adults. I need to know what happened…and I need your help," he finished, hoping the appeal would stir something in her. He could understand that she might not want to see him, but there were too many unanswered questions for him to take no for an answer.

After a seemingly eternal pause, the lock rattled and the door creaked open. It was dark in the small living room, all the drapes pulled, he saw as Jasmine padded in bare feet back to the chair in front of the television and sat. She was wearing a nightgown even though it was close to noon. It was so dim that he could hardly make her out.

"Can we turn on a light or open a window? I can't see my own hand in front of me."

"I…I'm comfortable with it like this. This is my house now, so I keep it the way I like. If you have a problem with it, leave," Jasmine advised in a monotone.

What the hell was going on here? Even after two years, people didn't change that much. What had happened?

"Jasmine. No problem. You want it dark, I like it dark. Can we start over? Tell me what happened to your father, Emilio. Please. Start at the beginning. I haven't had any news since I left."

"I see you have a uniform. Marines. Is that what happened to you? You ran away and joined the navy?

That's classic. A total cliché," she exclaimed with a bitter laugh.

"It's a little more complicated than that. But tell me about your father."

Jasmine let out a long sigh, and sank further into the large, padded reclining chair – one of Emilio's few luxuries; a place he could relax at the end of a long, hard day and watch some television in peace.

"When you left, you got out just in time. Someone executed *Don* Miguel, as well as one of his lieutenants, either that same day or the day after. I don't really remember now, so much happened so quickly. Anyway, nobody knew what to do, and it was chaos here. But word traveled fast, because before *Don* Miguel was in the ground, his rivals where fighting over how his empire would be divided up. It quickly escalated into the usual blood feud, and soon Culiacan's streets were littered with the dead," Jasmine explained.

Only the young man knew what had transpired between himself and *Don* Miguel before leaving the state – the event hadn't been witnessed by anyone, and nobody had any reason to suspect the quiet boy who was like his son. After the drug lord had disappeared, in the chaos that followed no one had much cared what had happened to the boy.

"And your father?"

"One night, several trucks showed up at the house, and we heard gunfire. The main contender for the *Don*'s position, Armand Altamar, had decided to eliminate anyone who was still loyal to the *Don*, in a bid to seal his position as the new *jefe* for this region. He executed the few remaining staff at the house...and then he came for us. My father had several guns and he tried to defend us, and even killed three of Altamar's henchmen, but in the end it was for nothing. There were too many of them, and they shot him to death, out in front of the porch...like a dog. He died there for no reason other than for loyalty to his boss – Altamar had no reason to kill him, but he did anyway, without as much thought as stepping on an ant. Papa...he wasn't even in the business. He just ran the horses, and raised you...," her voice trailed off.

"Jasmine, I'm so sorry. I...I don't know what to say..."

"There's nothing to say. After killing him, they broke down the door, dragged my grandmother and auntie outside and shot them in the head."

"Good God. I...thank God you escaped..."

"But I didn't, don't you see? I tried to shoot them but I was shaking too much, and my first shot missed. So then they came for me...and the rest...is history," she said flatly.

"What happened, Jasmine. You can tell me." He didn't know how to react to the horrible story and was afraid to hear the rest but he couldn't help himself.

"What happened? What happened? With nobody here to protect me, with you gone and my family killed? They took turns raping me, is what happened – over and over, for half the night. I passed out, and when I came to, they were raping me more. It went on for hours."

"I...Jasmine. I know nothing I can say or do will make anything better. But I'll find these men and punish them for what they did to you. They'll pay, with interest added."

"Just go. I don't want your help. My life is over before it had a chance to really begin. It's not your fault but I don't want to see you ever again. You remind me of before…when I had hope…"

"Jasmine, listen to me. There's still hope. I know what happened was horrible and will stay with you forever but there's always hope. Always. I'll make this right, or at least avenge your family and you," the young man promised.

"No you won't. And no, there's no hope. Trust me. None."

"There's always hope, Jasmine—"

"You're an idiot. For you, maybe there is, but not for me. I didn't finish the story. You didn't let me. After they were done with me, every orifice brutalized and bleeding, the leader, Altamar, went into the barn and got some of the acid they used on the glass tiles in the fountain – to remove the calcium deposits, as I remember. They'd always wear gloves, and mix it fifty parts water to one part acid. It was the only thing that would remove the buildup. Altamar didn't wear gloves, and he didn't mix it. He just poured it on my face, laughing as my skin fizzed with screaming agony. Last thing I remember was trying to make it to the kitchen to rinse it off my face with water. That probably saved my life." She stopped and peered at him through the gloom. "I wish they'd killed me. I've sat here many times, ever since they released me from the hospital, wishing I was dead. I'd kill myself but it would damn my soul to hell forever, according to the priest who stops in occasionally to mitigate my torment. So I sit in the dark, and pray to an unlikely god to end my misery. So far, he's ignored me, just the same as he ignored my family's cries for mercy."

"Jesus…"

"There's no Jesus here. There's only what they turned me into. What they did to me. There's only this."

Jasmine leaned forward so that he could see her face in the dim light. One side was the Jasmine he remembered. Beautiful, serene, now with tears streaming freely down her cheek. The other side of her face was an abomination. The acid had seared off her living flesh, blinded her, and so ruined it that it more resembled something that had been dragged down a road for miles, or trapped in a fire, than something human. The tendons and ligaments were exposed and, even two years after the horrific event, it was a suppurating wet sore...a picture of hell on earth incarnate. The young man had seen plenty of death and savagery in his life but even he was shocked, and he automatically recoiled from the sight. It was the most horrible thing he'd ever seen. He felt his gag reflex triggering as the pit of his stomach dropped out.

"Oh... Oh God, Jasmine..."

There was nothing to say. No words anyone could say to make it better.

Jasmine had been right.

There was no hope.

CHAPTER 7

The cantina lights twinkled in the softness of the spring night air; the bouncing beat of lively Banda music floated out from inside, along with raucous laughter and peals of glee from inebriated women. It was Saturday night and the party was in full swing on the outskirts of Culiacan, a rough and rural area populated by hard men with dead eyes and females who were looking for a fast luxury ride to nowhere. This was cartel country and the bar was a cartel bar, so if you hadn't grown up in the area and didn't know the owners, you didn't go inside unless you had a death wish.

It was one of the few places in Mexico where Armand Altamar could let his hair down and relax. He wasn't at war with anyone for the time being so he had little to fear. Things were prospering under his iron rule and everyone was making a ton of money since he'd taken over most of *Don* Miguel's duties. He'd had to give up some of the meth and heroin traffic to Diego up north, and had to cut in Aranas, the head of the Sinaloa cartel, for a fifteen-percent-larger slice of his cocaine traffic; but even so, business had grown to the point where he didn't even feel the dilution – he was pocketing fifty million dollars a month, on a bad one.

Not so bad for a forty-year-old ex-enforcer who had come up from the streets, fighting tooth and nail for anything he ever got. He'd been born in one of Culiacan's worst barrios, a desperate den of poverty and filth that few walked away from. Now he was running things after someone had taken out the *Don*. It was like a dream come true and he was making the most of it. Every weekend, he would hire one of the most popular Banda groups in Sinaloa to play for his de facto private party at his bar. Every friend he had would attend, as well as some of the most beautiful examples of Mexican femininity in the country – all to pay homage to him and celebrate his success.

Not that winning the spoils had been easy, by any means. For a few months after the *Don* had passed on to his just reward, Culiacan had been a death zone. Five or six different factions fought it out for his turf, and the streets had literally run red with their blood. The only way Altamar had emerged victorious was through a combination of epic brutality, stealth, deceit and, surprisingly, a willingness to compromise with his rivals. After several of his competitors had been found beheaded, along with their entire families – including newborn babies, aged relatives and even household pets – the notion of doing a deal to end the madness had been appealing to even the most battle-hardened contenders. And so a cautious truce had gone into effect. The killing stopped, prosperity returned and everyone went back to doing what they were supposed to do: making money – a lot of money. Maybe not as much as if one man ran it all, as *Don* Miguel had, but, then again, more than anyone could spend in a hundred lifetimes, just the same.

Altamar had introduced the idea that you had to be alive to spend it, and had been utterly ruthless in driving home the point that, unless you cooperated and stepped out of the way, your life wasn't worth anything. Over four hundred and seventy people had lost their lives in the two months following the *Don*'s passing, at least according to the official count. The actual number was more like double that, many left rotting in hidden fields for the carrion birds to pick apart, or buried in shallow graves. One particularly brutal week, the rivers had been chocked with bodies floating down from the marijuana fields. It finally got to the point where even those accustomed to incredible violence and brutality had been through enough, and so they worked out a truce.

He'd proved his point. If you crossed him, you, your family, your servants and their families would all be slaughtered without a second's hesitation. It had been a stunningly effective campaign. By its short but bloody end, he was in charge of a coalition of former rivals – who were all still alive to spend their money. True, he'd made lifelong enemies due to his tactics, but he wasn't worried. Nobody dared move against him. The price of even the slightest thing going wrong was the extermination of everyone you knew, of everything you held precious. The stakes were just too high, so he settled into his position of power with confidence, while always sleeping with one eye open.

His entourage were the most dangerous and violent killers in the region; he made a huge point of advertising that fact. They were men who drank baby blood for breakfast and killed priests over coffee. By cultivating the reputation as the devil walking the earth, he'd climbed to the pinnacle of his world; the view from up top was better than he'd ever expected. He had his pick of the most gorgeous young women, he was literally awash with cash and every comfort and toy he desired. He was feared and revered for his ruthlessness and his absolute power. It was as close as you could get to being a demigod.

And it was good.

Tonight, he'd been drinking tequila with his cousins, who were never far away from his side. He surrounded himself with family and made sure they also wanted for nothing. Blood was their bond, he'd repeat over and over when drunk. Altamar made sure that they understood he was a hundred percent loyal to his family, and he expected nothing less in return but the same. The threat was as clear as the reward. Stick with Altamar, and you would live a happy and prosperous life. Get it into your head to betray him and he'd erase you from the earth.

The combination of carrot and stick was highly effective.

Inside the club, the air was thick with a haze of cigarette and marijuana smoke. The police avoided the building like it was radioactive, so there were no rules when within its four walls, the interior of which were covered with cowboy regalia. Lassos, bridles, photos of prize bulls and horses, horseshoes. Myriad related paraphernalia adorned every inch of the place, giving it an air of a themed junk shop. Booths ringed both of the longer sides of the room, which featured an elaborate stage on one end and a long wooden bar on the opposite. Girls in cowboy hats and microscopic jean shorts or miniskirts and cowboy boots weaved their way between the small circular tables that cluttered half the floor – the remainder of which was left to the many dancers. The fifteen-piece band barely fitted on the stage but neither the musicians nor the celebrants seemed to mind as the caterwauling of the dissonant horn section battled with the strident tenor of the singer, who was belting out a song begging apology for a series of indiscretions with other women; because this time, he'd be faithful due to having changed. Straw was scattered about the floor in an effort to create a more authentically rustic experience. The overall tone of the establishment was a rowdy rural roadhouse, albeit fifteen minutes from the edge of a cosmopolitan city of over a million in population.

Most of the men wore jeans or slacks with cowboy boots and hats; their female companions wore little but smiles, their modesty cloaked by strategically-donned tops that struggled to contain their charms, with shorts or pants that looked like they'd been sprayed on. Many of the girls were in their late teens to early twenties – with a fair mix of professionals and those looking to find a generous *narcotraficante* sugar daddy. It was a playground for men who lived at breakneck speed, for whom the light of tomorrow was not guaranteed, and who denied themselves nothing.

Outside the building, four discreetly armed men loitered a few feet from the entrance, providing the obligatory muscle should anyone be so foolhardy as to interrupt the *fiesta* with unpleasantness. They were in their mid-twenties, with a palpable air of menace and dispositions that indicated their willingness to kill you just as readily as bum a smoke. Two were ex-marines, the other two survivors of a lifetime on the street – the four of them had tallied between themselves at least ten times their number in killings.

The area around the club was dense brush that had been cleared to create the mammoth dirt parking lot. A custom-built neon sign atop a metal column blinked the image of a highly-stylized devil wearing a cowboy hat and leering suggestively at new arrivals, its oscillating illumination lending a carnival air to the tightly parked cars. Occasionally, another vehicle would pull off the main road and brave the hundred yards to the club, headlights briefly shining on the front of the establishment before finding a spot among the rest of the patrons.

Inside, Altamar slammed his fist down on the scarred table-top of his favorite booth, having just finished telling another tale of one of his conquests, and threw back his head and laughed with delight. The girls on either side of him were all smiles. Another round of tequila and beer hastily arrived, Altamar having waved down a waitress moments earlier. The service staff didn't need to ask what kind – it was always the same. Negra Modelo and *Cazadores*. Altamar liked the familiar, and he was a veritable drinking machine every Friday and Saturday night. His cousins invariably struggled to keep up with him as the hour got late, which deterred him not one iota. He'd be having a private party later with the pair of youthful minxes accompanying him. His two cousins eyed him with envious admiration even as their vision began to blur. They had their own girls, but not much was going to be happening by the end of the night, when they'd fall dazed into bed with the room spinning while their companions did their best to entertain them. Altamar, on the other hand, had a reputation for being insatiable, more than likely helped by the plentiful chemical supplementation he lavished upon himself. He looked around after delivering the hysterically funny punch-line to his latest story, and delivered it again, louder, for emphasis. No doubt it would be even funnier the second time.

"So I tell the fucker, 'What, you think you're superman? All right, asshole, so you'll have no problem flying.' And then I threw him off the roof of the building. You know, in the end, he didn't fly so good!" He pounded the table again, killing himself with his wit.

His company tittered drunkenly, the girls beaming toothy smiles, but he quickly lost interest in the ladies as nature called. Altamar stood up unsteadily and, after stabilizing himself with the table, woozily moved to the rear of the club, where he had an office with a private restroom. He grappled with his keys and unlocked the door before entering and turning the deadbolt, ensuring he wouldn't be interrupted while conducting his important business. Altamar flicked on the overhead light and leaned against the wall for a second, as though the act of walking forty yards had sapped his energy. Maybe he'd had too much tequila too fast, he thought, and then he stumbled over to his desk, slid the center drawer open and extracted a small vial. He fiddled with the top, and after tearing it free tapped out two fat lines of cocaine on the glass desktop. He rolled up a hundred dollar bill and snorted them with gusto, wincing at the delicious burn as the drug hit his septum. Augmentation complete, he moved to the bathroom and opened the door. He failed to notice the shadow in the dark room or the quiet rustle before excruciating pain lanced through his head and everything went dark.

Fifteen minutes later, his cousins realized that Altamar had been gone a long time and staggered back to the office to check on him. The door was locked, which wasn't unexpected. The men pounded on it, calling to him. After getting no response to multiple efforts, they went and found two of Altamar's security detail, who swiftly broke the door down, guns drawn. The office was pitch black. When they turned on the lights, they were confronted with an empty room. The most sober of the cousins went to the window and pulled the blinds up, then yelled at the two guards, pointing at the opening.

Three of the iron bars over the window had been cut, either with a welding torch or some sort of acid, and were bent out at right angles, creating a space just large enough for a body to fit through.

The music stopped two minutes later. The *fiesta* was abruptly terminated. Armed men milled about, uncertain as to what to do until the cousin who had discovered the window issued instructions and they raced for their vehicles.

Altamar faded in and out of consciousness, unsure what was happening to him. He was bouncing against a hard surface, felt cool air blowing over him and a sense of motion. He struggled to move but his wrists and ankles were bound and he had tape over his mouth. He opened his eyes wider but couldn't make anything out; something was blocking his vision. His arm hurt in the upper bicep like he'd been shot, and the last thought he had as he faded again was that someone had injected him with something to knock him out.

Eventually, Altamar returned to full awareness and this time he could see, albeit without much clarity. He blinked his eyes in a futile effort to clear his head, which was splitting from the blow. He tried to reach up to touch the tender spot and discovered that he could only move his arm a few inches from where it was extended slightly above shoulder level. He tried the other arm, also extended, and met with the same resistance. Now fully alert, his respiration increased and he was flooded with a sense of panic. When he tried to move his legs, he encountered the same problem – he was immobilized, spread-eagled, his arms and legs stretched wide. His nose registered the musty odor of long-abandoned horse stalls, and when his vision returned to near normal, he could see that he was indeed in an old barn, chained to the floor. He continued to struggle for a few minutes until blood began tricking from his wrists where he'd torn most of the skin off from pulling against the chains.

Dim light came from a pair of headlights outside the closed barn door, where slim illumination crept through from around the sides and the base. Altamar screamed, more a hoarse croak than anything, largely due to the effects on his vocal cords of whatever he'd been dosed with. He paused after several seconds and heard a sound from the far end of the space. He was able to move his head and crane his neck and he saw a young man dressed entirely in black turn to face him from the area by the stalls. The young man sauntered over unhurriedly and smiled humorlessly at Altamar, causing his breath to catch in his throat and his blood to run cold. He knew that look, and knew what it meant. He needed to take the initiative or this could get far worse.

"You fucking cocksucker. I'll cut your balls off and force you to eat them in front of me. Do you have any idea who I am?" Altamar rasped at him. A good defense was often a strong offense.

The young man smiled again, almost blithely, and without responding, opened the barn door and sauntered out to the truck that was parked outside, returning after a few minutes with a lit kerosene lantern. He placed it carefully on a stall ledge so it brightened the area where Altamar was chained and went back to the truck, extinguishing its headlights and shutting off the motor. Altamar heard the man's footsteps grow louder and then he was blinded by a blue-white flash. His vision gradually returned, and he was blinded by another.

The young man was taking photographs of him.

A spike of fear ran through Altamar. He decided to try a different approach.

"I'm very, very rich. I can get you whatever you want, eh? Anything. How much money do you want? What's it going to take?" Altamar sensed that threats weren't going to have any effect, so he'd appeal to greed, which was a constant in all humans. It wasn't a question of if, it was a matter of how much.

The man just smiled again, shaking his head as if dealing with a child.

"Did you hear me? I can get you anything. Millions of dollars. In cash. What's your number? What do you want? A million? Two million? Fine. I can get you two million dollars with a phone call."

The young man considered the idea, and then nodded.

"I think I'd like to be a millionaire. That sounds like it would be fun. So you get me two million dollars, and then once I have the money and I'm safe, I'll release you. I'll unlock your chains, and you'll be free to go. You don't know me, so I'm not worried about being found by your thugs. How do we do this?" the young man asked.

"Now you're thinking. In my pocket. I have a phone. Get it for me, and I'll give you a number to call. Let me talk, and we'll set up getting you your money."

"But how? How will I get the money and know I'm safe, and that your men aren't watching me or following me?" he asked.

"We can do it like I've done some of my deals. We pick a remote location you're familiar with. At a predetermined time, a man will come and put a bag with the money wherever you like, and then leave. You wait as long as you want, and then retrieve the money. It's a standard drop. We do it all the time," Altamar explained.

"Ah. Good thinking. I think I can improve on that. I have an idea that will work."

And then he explained what he wanted.

Altamar's eyes widened. "Very smart. I've never heard of anything like that before. I see what you're trying to do. It will be impossible to follow you that way. Okay, make the call. We have a deal. You get your money, you unchain me and let me go, right? I'm a man of my word. How will I know you'll do as you say?"

"I went to a lot of trouble to get you out alive. If I'd wanted to kill you, you'd have been dead an hour ago. I want something else. So make the call, and let's get this over with," the young man replied.

Altamar's features clouded – something about the interaction was off. He didn't know what, but he didn't believe his captor. "You know what? Fuck you. I think you're lying, and you're going to kill me anyway," he hissed.

"Fair enough. I guess I'll kill you now. And you'll never find out if you were wrong." The young man shrugged, apparently uninterested in which way the transaction went. From the back of his pants, he pulled a semi-automatic pistol and approached Altamar.

The drug lord struggled to maintain his composure, but his eyes widened at the sight of the gun. "Wait. Here's my proposal. You get the two million, but you hand me over in exchange for the money when you get it."

The young man smiled again with genuine amusement.

"I must not be very convincing, or you must be very stupid. This isn't a negotiation. You either give me two million dollars on my terms, and I release you, or you fuck around and I blow your brains out. Or maybe I gut shoot you and watch you lie in your own shit and blood for a few hours while you beg me to end the agony." He considered that mental image. "You really think I'm going to let your men pick me off with a sniper rifle the second you're safe? I'm disappointed. I was sure you were smarter than that. Maybe I'll blow your kneecaps off, and you'll be walking around on prosthetic limbs for the rest of your miserable life, just so you know I'm serious. Do you need me to do that? Show you I'm serious?"

Altamar hesitated, calculating, and then his shoulders slumped.

"No. I believe you. Fine. We'll do it your way. Make the call."

The young man dialed the number Altamar gave him, and then held the phone up to the ear of the cartel kingpin. When the other end of the line answered, Altamar explained he'd been kidnapped, but that it was okay, and to gather two million in cash and have it ready to go at four a.m. – in two more hours. He then gave instructions on how it was to be delivered. Altamar had many millions in cash stashed in multiple places in town, so getting two million was the least of his problems.

Altamar listened to the response and then barked angrily into the phone.

"Don't argue with me. Just do it. My life is at stake here. Do it precisely as I explained, and don't fuck around or try anything clever. I don't want to die because you got smart," Altamar warned, before the young man terminated the call and pocketed the phone. "All right. I did my part. So now you go get your money, and then you let me go. You better move a long way away from here, because it's not going to be very healthy for you after this, you know?" Altamar couldn't resist the threat. He had a good sense for people, and he believed that the young man would release him.

"I don't intend to stay very long. Now, if you'll excuse me, I have some things to attend to," the young man apologized, turning to leave.

Altamar was startled by a sound of scurrying from out of his field of vision, above his head.

"What the fuck? What's that?" he hissed.

"That? Oh, that's probably the rats, I expect. I remember the place was infested with them last time I was here," the young man said conversationally.

"Rats? Then you can't leave me here on the ground. Get me up," Altamar demanded.

The young man appeared to consider it.

"No, you'll stay where you are. Besides, you'll soon have bigger things to think about than a few pesky rats," he reasoned, and moved to grab the bottle he'd placed on the ground near the door.

"What's that?" Altamar asked, his voice catching.

"You'll know soon enough. I wanted to leave you something to reflect upon while I'm off picking up my money. You may not remember, but you hurt someone I care deeply about and I'm here to return the favor. That was why I wanted you alive, although once you made the offer of the money, I felt it would be poor manners to turn it down," the young man explained, carefully unscrewing the top of the glass bottle.

Altamar stared up at him, horrified, as the young man approached. He renewed his struggle against the chains. "No. You promised you'd let me go," Altamar protested.

"I did. And I will. But I never promised you'd want to be let go," he said, and then poured a small amount of the acid on the cartel boss' face, careful to avoid splashing any on his own clothes or shoes. Altamar's skin began to bubble and smoke, and his eyes immediately ulcerated as the fluid seared through the lids. Altamar's agonized shrieks were bloodcurdling, but had no effect on the young man. They were in the middle of nowhere, the big house abandoned and Jasmine's home a quarter mile away. There was no one to hear the screams, which gradually died as some acid entered his mouth and cauterized his tongue and throat. The young man resealed the bottle and placed it on the stall next to the lantern, and then turned, unbuckling his pants.

"I'd rape your sorry ass as well, but I'm afraid I'd catch something. So instead, I'll leave you to the rats. They'll come soon enough," he disclosed as he urinated on Altamar's face, rinsing off most of the acid so the man would remain alive. He wanted the agony to last as long as possible, and he didn't want the scumbag to get off lightly by dying after a few minutes of unspeakable pain.

"I'll be back after I get the money you so generously offered. I should have held out for five, but since it's not about the money, two is more than enough – no point in being greedy, and it would be harder to carry. When I get back, if the rats have left anything of you, I'll release you just as I promised. Without a face, but then again, you've done as bad or worse, so you can't really complain," he reasoned.

Altamar gurgled, choking. It was now hard to tell given the condition of what had been his face, but the young man thought he might be choking, the acid having removed his nose along with most of his skin and tendons. He reached into his back pocket and withdrew a pocket knife, which he opened as he approached the drug boss. Kneeling down, he stabbed it into the man's windpipe just above his clavicle, and then stepped back to study the wound. Blood frothed forth, and he turned and trotted out to the truck, returning a few seconds later with a pen. He used his teeth to pull out the ballpoint mechanism, leaving a slender tube, which he first blew through, and then jabbed through the bloody opening. He listened attentively, and was rewarded with the sound of air moving in and out through the pen, albeit labored breathing – but beggars couldn't be choosers.

"There. You'll live. Although you'll wish you hadn't. I'll be taking the lantern. The rats seem to prefer the dark for their work. They seem emboldened by the night. Have a nice rest," he said, and then grabbed the light and walked out of the barn, taking care to shut the door securely behind him. The big Ford Lobo engine started, and the last thing Altamar registered as the wheels crunched on the gravel outside was the sound of the exhaust disappearing in the distance.

Then the rats came.

CHAPTER 8

A green Ford Explorer pulled into the darkened lot of the little restaurant. A man got out, carrying a backpack with two million dollars in it, carefully sealed in Ziploc freezer bags. After surveying the road and verifying he was alone, he swung the rear of the SUV open and withdrew an inflated tire inner tube. He strapped the backpack securely to the tire using two bungee cords and stuck a cheap plastic flashlight into the exterior flap of the bag, the lens sticking out partway. He gingerly carried the ensemble down the banks to the edge of the *Canal Rosales*, and scanning the area again, flicked the switch on the flashlight before putting the inner tube on the water's surface and pushing it out towards the middle of the moving current. He watched as it floated slowly away from him to the middle of the fifty-foot-wide canal, the little light bobbing as it made its way downstream. Once it was out of sight, he returned to his truck and drove away.

The young man spied on him from a hundred yards downstream through binoculars, noting the passage of the floating treasure as it moved slowly by him, and watched the man's tail lights disappear down the road. Once he was satisfied that he was alone he ran down the overgrown bank as far as he could make it, before diving into the canal. Within a few minutes his powerful strokes had carried him downstream, and he caught up to the tire. He switched off the flashlight so he would be completely invisible in the dark, moonless night. He made for the shore, and once close began moving against the current to a concrete embankment he'd drifted forty yards beyond. After reaching the bank he exited the chilly water, pausing to remove the backpack from the contrivance before lashing the flashlight back in place on the tube, switching it back on, and pushing it out into the stream again, on the off chance they'd been stupid enough to position someone further downstream at the bridge that spanned the canal a quarter mile away.

He moved into the brush and located his black army boots exactly where he'd left them, with a change of dry clothes. He quickly stripped off his soaking black T-shirt and pants and wrung them out before stuffing them into the bag with the cash. After slipping into another black shirt and a pair of jeans, he pulled his boots on and was ready to move within two minutes. He edged silently through the brush and found the path at the end of which he'd left the truck, and debated his next move.

There was more to attend to. He'd need to keep his word and deal with Altamar. He started the engine, and then had a thought so evil it surprised even him. There was a sense of poetic justice to it, really.

He put the big truck in gear and pulled off into the night, tapping his fingers to the faint Latin rock beat playing on the radio. *So this was what it was like to be rich.*

Sort of cold and wet, but it would do.

By the time he made it back to the barn it was five-thirty in the morning, and dawn would be shining its rays onto the valley within forty-five minutes. He wanted to make short work of his remaining chores, so he sprang from the truck and moved to the barn entrance, carrying the lantern with him as he whistled a happy tune. When he opened the door he was greeted by angry squeaking from a mass of rats that were feeding on Altamar, most of which scurried away in fear when he swung the lantern at them.

He inspected the feared cartel chief's ravaged torso and face, checking for signs of breathing, and was rewarded by his chest laboring to draw air through the tube. He shook his head – it was truly amazing that he'd made it. The scumbag had the constitution of an ox.

The young man crouched down, unlocked the padlocks that secured the chains on the drug lord's feet and hands, and left them by his side. He stood, surveying the barn's interior, and saw that there was still abundant desiccated hay on the floor. Altamar emitted a groaning sound from where his mouth had been, but where now there were merely gums and teeth, his lips having been neatly removed by the acid…and then the rats. The young man fished the camera out again and took another photo, ensuring that the time stamp wasn't on.

"I'm back. A deal's a deal. I released you. I think that it's a safe bet that with a mug like that you won't be doing the cover shot for *TeleNoticias* any time soon, but maybe you can get some part-time work scaring kids for Halloween. You're free to go, so thanks for the memories and have a nice life. Oh, and I know you'll need some light given the condition of what's left of your eyes, so I'll be a nice guy and leave the lantern burning for you. Hope you make it out before the fire gets out of control. That's got to be a horrible way to die," the young man said in a kind, soft voice, before tossing the lantern against the ground and watching the kerosene splatter onto the dry hay from its broken reservoir. The fire immediately spread and began to roar, and soon the entire barn was ablaze.

Inspecting his work with quiet satisfaction, the young man spun and walked to the door, pausing to kick Altamar in the groin as he moved past him. It wouldn't do to have the filthy parasite passing out. He'd want his full attention for this phase of what remained of his short life.

The fire licked from the barn door and windows as he started the truck's engine. After a few moments it was obvious that Altamar wasn't going to make it out. A shame, really. It would almost be better if he somehow managed to survive. A life in that mangled condition would be fitting punishment for what he'd done to Jasmine and her family.

But a deal was a deal, and he'd kept his word.

He slid the transmission into reverse and pulled away.

There was nothing left to see.

The truck approached the small house and rolled to a stop, the engine going silent as the driver-side door opened. The young man moved to the home's entrance and expertly picked the lock. Once inside, he crept soundlessly to the main bedroom, where Jasmine was sleeping.

He'd been tortured since he'd seen her face. Even after getting revenge for the vicious brutality, he knew her life was going to continue to be a miserable nightmare.

Nobody could help her. He'd gladly leave her the two million dollars if he thought for a second that medicine could fix her face to anything resembling normalcy, but he knew that was an impossibility. It was just another example of a cruel and unpredictable universe punishing the innocents and making their every moment a tortured farce.

He watched as she lay, breathing fitfully, her ravaged profile a constant reminder of the pain she'd endured, and then he pulled his pistol from his belt and shot her in the head.

Ten minutes later he sat on the hood of the truck, watching the house burn, embers blowing into the pre-dawn as they carried his Jasmine's soul with them. He reasoned that if there was such thing as hell, he would be going anyway, so he was more than willing to carry the burden of ending her suffering and doing what she couldn't do for herself. He winced as the roof collapsed, the propane for the stove having provided ample fuel to get the blaze started. A single tear trickled its way down his cheek — his lonely offering to a world that brutalized its children and savaged its meek. His shoulders shuddered as he cried for what could have been, and what Jasmine could have had, at the unfairness of it all and the pointlessness of everything.

Eventually, his sorrow exhausted, he gruffly rubbed the moisture from his face with his shirt sleeve before getting behind the wheel and driving away. There was still much to be done, and he could bemoan his existence later.

Solomon Valiente sat in the office of his furniture store, *ranchero* music humming forth from the showroom speakers in an attempt to lure pedestrians in, wondering what the gimmick was in this overture from an unknown. He'd gotten a strange call an hour earlier indicating that a stranger wanted to speak with him on an important matter of urgency. He rubbed his neck, absently fingering the heavy gold links that held the crucifix he never removed. He gestured to the two men standing by his door to allow the young man to enter his office.

Valiente was one of the main rivals to Altamar's iron hold on his empire, and it was well known that he hated the drug lord, furious over some close family members who had been killed by Altamar's goons when the power struggle over *Don* Miguel's holdings was underway. In the interests of prosperity they'd made their fragile pact, but Valiente held a grudge, and he was a dangerous and powerful adversary in his own right.

The young man had approached him through a street-level enforcer that morning and requested a meeting. He claimed to have something of tremendous value to offer Valiente, which had naturally piqued his interest – Valiente was a man best avoided, so he wasn't accustomed to being solicited for anything. Three security men had frisked the young man upon his arrival, verifying that he had no weapons and wasn't wearing a wire before allowing him near Valiente's office; so there could be no trickery or immediate physical threat – always a concern in the cartel game, where you could routinely expect attempts on your life on virtually any pretense.

Valiente leaned forward in his reclining chair as the young man entered and sat in one of the two chairs in front of his desk, a stern, armed enforcer bracketing him on either side, ever mindful of the slightest wrong move.

"So, you want a meeting. Here it is. Tell me what it is you have that's of such value to me," Valiente started, sipping his coffee while appraising the young man's face.

"I'm an ex-marine. I want to begin a career as a specialist in contract executions for your cartel. I've been trained in every sort of weapons and demolition, and I have a year's worth of combat experience with over thirty-six confirmed kills," the young man began.

"That's interesting, but it's not of that much value to me. Don't get me wrong, I can always use good men, but there's a difference between coming looking for a job, and bringing me something of value," Valiente observed.

"I know. And I'm not looking for a job. I'm offering my services as a contractor. And what I have to offer you, I believe, is significant. As a good faith token, take a look at this. It was taken seven hours ago." He removed the small digital camera from his pants pocket, powered it on and thumbed through the photos until he reached the desired one. He handed the device to Valiente.

Valiente peered at the screen and blinked, and then his eyes narrowed, taking on a vaguely reptilian cast.

"Both of you. Get out," he instructed his bodyguards. The two hulking men exchanged glances, and then with distrustful glares at the new arrival, obediently left the room.

"I could have you killed for this, and Altamar would reward me with anything I wanted."

"No. He wouldn't. He can't give you what you really want. Only I can. Today. Because you don't want to live in his shadow forever, and I have the ability to make him disappear, now, and never give you any more problems. You and you alone would know he was gone, enabling you to consolidate power and take steps ahead of any of your competitors, ensuring that you'd replace him. Here's what I propose. You pay me three hundred thousand dollars and he disappears effective immediately." Valiente's eyes tracked the young man's unblinking gaze as he spoke. "You pay me two hundred thousand dollars each for as many of your rivals you want dispatched within the next seventy-two hours, and I'll make it so. It's a guarantee that you will take over Altamar's business at that point, which will make you that amount of money in a matter of minutes. I have him right now, so you haven't attempted anything. I have. As I see it, you have nothing to lose and everything to gain." The young man had spoken in a calm, soft voice, with measured inflection, laying out the options in a methodical manner.

Valiente sank back into his plush chair and considered the proposition while eying the young man. He weighed the options and then rose.

"If you can do this, we have a deal. What payment do you propose?"

"The three hundred I want now, and before the day's end I will bring you a photo of your enemy dead. The others, half up front, half upon successful completion. It's actually a bargain, but I'm anxious to make a name for myself and earn your support," the young man said.

Valiente nodded. It was indeed a bargain. They both knew it. He was being handed the keys to the kingdom for a song.

"I have to say, this comes as a complete surprise. If you can pull this off, you'll be very, very busy carrying out jobs for me." Valiente stared into his empty cup. "And what is your name? What shall I call you, my young mystery killer who comes bearing gifts?"

The young man didn't hesitate. He'd already decided on his professional moniker. He would be named after the cursed card that had ruined his life, and had freed him at the same time.

"*El Rey*. After the tarot card, the King of Swords. You can call me *El Rey*."

CHAPTER 9

Later that evening, after catching a few hours of sleep, *El Rey* returned to Valiente with the photo of Altamar after the acid facial scrub, having collected his fee before departing the office earlier in the day. The cartel boss was both fascinated and repelled by the 'after' image of Altamar – and this was a man who saw death on an almost daily basis.

"Jesus Christ. What did you do to him?" Valiente exclaimed.

El Rey shrugged. "Acid."

"Damn, kid. You're one sick bastard, I'll grant you that. I never want to piss you off," Valiente admitted.

"I figured you'd want something that would make a statement. You can download the photo or I can e-mail it to you for circulation purposes if anyone ever decides to test your power. I imagine it would deliver a considerable deterrent value," *El Rey* said.

"This will stop anyone that doesn't have a death wish in their tracks." Valiente slid a folder to him, along with a black garbage bag. "I have three primary rivals I need executed in the next two days. Their details are in the folder. Half the money for the first contract is in the sack.

Come back when you've done the first one and I'll pay you the balance and give you a payment for the second and third contracts. But I need this handled quickly, because once they get wise to Altamar being missing for any significant period of time they'll be coming for me."

"Then I better get going. I could use some help locating a few things for the jobs, though. I figure you'd know where to find these." He handed Valiente a small piece of notepaper. "The sooner I can get them, the sooner I can fulfill these contracts."

Valiente studied the precisely detailed list.

"The M4 is no problem. We've got a bunch of those. Don't know if any have a night scope on them, though. Let me make a call. The Remington we also have, or can get within a few hours. Same for the Beretta with a silencer. Pretty standard issue, that." Valiente looked up from the list and *El Rey* nodded approvingly. "Lot of the marines bring those Remington 700s with them – they love their sniper rifles. I see you're okay with the .308. That will make it easy. Oh, and plastique and grenades? How messy do you plan to make this? I don't want to be associated with public bloodbaths in crowds. You need to be surgical."

"I intend to be as discreet as possible, but it's better to be prepared, than not. For now, I'll get busy on the first contract while you source that gear. How can I contact you at night? I'll want to pick up the weapons as soon as you have them."

Valiente scribbled a cell number on the back of a card.

"Call me in two hours and we'll arrange a drop-off. Don't worry about the cost; they're on me. I'm presuming you'll want, what, five hundred rounds for the M4 and maybe fifty for the Remington and the Beretta?" Valiente confirmed.

El Rey nodded. "Make it a hundred for the Beretta."

Valiente grunted. He was already imagining how it would feel to be sitting on Altamar's throne.

"Okay, then, we're set. And you, my friend, can call me any time." He looked at the image on the little camera again. "I'm glad you're on my side… '*El Rey*'."

"So am I."

Both men smiled, any humor never reaching their eyes.

El Rey had checked into a high-end hotel in town and now sat at the small rectangular table in his room going over the details of the three targets. He didn't see a problem taking them out but it would get progressively harder as word of a purge spread. Ideally, he would do all in the same night but the logistics wouldn't accommodate that, and he reconciled himself that he'd be lucky to get two, with the third on the schedule for the following day. He jotted the addresses down and decided to go for a drive to reconnoiter the neighborhoods and see what he would be dealing with. Valiente had supplied plentiful information on the targets' security, so there would hopefully be no surprises there, but he wanted to determine if there was anything Valiente had missed.

He would need a different vehicle than the truck, so he would have to buy something, preferably with an alarm and dependable, considering that he would be driving around with over two million in cash. It was a Thursday evening, so he headed to the part of town where all the new car dealers had lots, before they closed. Some lucky salesman was about to get a dream handed to him.

El Rey drove to the Toyota dealer, and after an hour emerged with the keys to a shiny new black 4 Runner with a factory alarm. That would more than do. He could do the reconnaissance in the plate-less Toyota and then use the big Ford for the actual hits. His days with the Ford were numbered in hours, so it would be best to use it, rather than the Toyota, for operational purposes.

He drove to the first target's ranch in a neighborhood on the outskirts of town, five acres with a nice colonial-style single-level house, a modest seven bedrooms per the information he'd been given. He knew from the photos and the file what to expect on the layout, and found several obvious holes in the security setup just driving by. The first target, Manuel Remarosa, would be a piece of cake.

The second hit wouldn't be so easy, he knew. The man lived an hour outside of Culiacan on a large parcel of land with only one entry – a heavily guarded private road. There was no point in driving out there before he picked up the weapons, so he returned to the hotel and called Valiente, who confirmed he had everything. They agreed to meet in half an hour at a restaurant in town and the hand-off went uneventfully. Valiente's security men kept a watchful eye out for threats as they chatted over a snack, before *El Rey* transferred the golf-bag with the weapons in it to the Lobo. After heading out to look at the second and third target's homes, he confirmed his instinct that he could only do two of the three that night, at best, and modified his strategy accordingly.

By the time he made it back to the hotel it was ten at night and he was tired, so after checking the weapons and loading them, he took a two hour cat-nap. The slumber did him a world of good, and by one a.m. he was parked a quarter mile from Manuel Remarosa's opulent home. He would use the Beretta and the M4 for this exercise, and hoped he'd be able to get in and out without having to fire the assault rifle. The pistol would be relatively silent; but opening up with an automatic rifle would draw considerable undesired attention.

El Rey was dressed from head to toe in dark gray army-surplus camouflage, nearly invisible as he slid silently through the brush on the periphery of the estate. He could make out the silhouettes of the armed guards sitting at their assigned points near the primary entry areas, but even so, he didn't anticipate any problems getting in and out. The one out on the breakfast patio was out of sight of the rest, so he was the weak link. *El Rey's* plan was to neutralize the man and then simply walk into the house, make his way to the target's bedroom and do the deed. It would be over in no time, before the gunmen had any idea what had happened.

The hurdle was how to cross the expanse of open space between the brush and the house without being detected. He'd need to time it perfectly so as to avoid getting into a firefight. This kind of spur of the moment operation depended entirely on the element of surprise. He preferred to plan his future hits carefully but he'd been handed the means by which to begin his career with a bang, so he'd do what needed to be done on these.

The problem was that, as he watched the house, he couldn't see any means to reach it without alarming the guard and bringing the full wrath of four armed men down on him. It sucked, but he would need to modify his plan to reflect reality. He'd thought that one of the angles would keep him hidden until he was almost right on the guard, but once he was in the brush he discovered that was illusory.

Calculating his next move, he hunkered down to wait, figuring it would be a long night.

Manuel Remarosa stretched on his four poster bed, and rolled over so that the morning light from the window wouldn't wake him up anymore than he already was. Sadie, his golden retriever, had other ideas and, hearing her master shift on the bed, decided it was time to send him a message of undying love in the form of sloppy wet kisses on his face. She jumped up onto the mattress between Manuel and his wife, Gloria, and firmly deposited herself, lavishing her beloved master with affection. Manuel swatted at her halfheartedly before rolling over again towards the window, resigned to his fate. He couldn't really get too angry with Sadie – she'd been sleeping on the bed with him since a tiny puppy of six weeks, and it was only since she turned one year old a few months ago and was now an adult that she'd been relegated to the terracotta tile of the floor.

"She loves you, *amor*. And you're the one who wanted a dog," Gloria murmured from her position on the bed, her voice thick with sleep.

"I know, I know. Don't get up. I'll take her out for a little exercise," Manuel replied sarcastically.

Gloria ignored the jab, already drifting back to dreamland. Manuel slid his slippers on and trundled across the floor to the bathroom, Sadie locked to his side in anticipation of going for a walk. He stood at the toilet going about his business, Sadie obediently waiting for him on the other side of the threshold to the forbidden area, and yawned loudly, stretching his arms over his head and finishing by rubbing his hand across the coarse stubble on his cheeks. He was fat, he knew, but not dangerously so; maybe forty or fifty pounds. But he could always lose it – that was his daily mantra before going for a half-hearted morning jog, which inevitably terminated with a huge breakfast loaded with cholesterol, carbs and cheese. Manuel scratched his bottom as he considered shaving, then decided he'd forego that chore today.

He entered the huge walk-in closet and donned his workout outfit – a green America soccer tunic and basketball shorts – before turning to Sadie, whose eyes twinkled with anticipation.

"Who wants to go for a walk?" he asked innocently.

Sadie danced back and forth, her tail whipping the air in a frenzy, doing everything in her power to convey to her master that it was she, indeed, that wanted to do so.

"If only I could find someone who wanted to go for a WALK!" Manuel exclaimed, and Sadie began whining as she pranced in the doorway, occasionally leaping into the air and twirling completely around in a canine display of balletic prowess.

Manuel decided to give the dog a break and not torture her any more, although he knew she enjoyed the buildup as much as he enjoyed her reaction. Together, they moved to the bedroom door and made their way down the hall, a wholly unlikely pair. He stopped in the kitchen and greeted Maria, their cook, who was already simmering something heavenly-smelling on the expansive Viking stove top.

"What's that?" he asked.

"Machaca, *Don* Remarosa," she replied softly. Maria was sixty, from Los Mochis, north of Culiacan on the Sea of Cortez, and was a remarkably talented cook. She'd been with him for a quarter of his forty years, and he still looked forward to her meals every day.

"Make sure it's low fat. Remember I'm on a diet," he chided, rubbing his ample belly with a grin.

"Always, *Don* Remarosa," Maria assured him.

Manuel was a brutal killer who had executed twenty competitors over his two decades of ascending the cartel ladder in Sinaloa, but he loved his mother, his four children, his dog, his wife and his two mistresses. And Maria's cooking.

It never occurred to him to question his lifestyle – he'd come up from the streets, where he'd started out as a collector for one of *Don* Aranas' cells, and had worked his way up to his current position as one of Altamar's trusted lieutenants, and was now making ten million dollars every year. This, for a boy from the slums who had terminated his education at the age of twelve to live by his wits on the streets of Culiacan. The cartel game had made him a rich man, and he wanted for nothing. If he had to get his hands dirty, so be it. He'd murdered his first man when he was thirteen, using a bread knife, and had never looked back.

His life had been relatively tranquil under the reign of his new boss, and he had hardly had to kill anyone so far this year – an anomaly for the business. It was a time of peace, and he was happy to be reaping the rewards of Altamar's rule. He still remembered the bad time a few years back when *Don* Miguel had been executed, the streets running red with blood. He'd had to pack his family and send them off to Lake Chapala during the worst of it. For months, he'd lived like a terrorist commander, hiding for his life in different anonymous locations as he waged a guerilla war against his competitors each day. It was like anything else, he supposed. There were good times and the not so good times. It wasn't perfect, but then again, nobody got rich in Mexico without getting bloody. He'd made his choices – and had prevailed. He couldn't complain.

Manuel lumbered to the entry door with Sadie springing alongside him and stepped outside to the crisp air of a bright new morning. He loved this time of day. It was cool enough so you weren't sweating through your clothes, and the rainy season hadn't started yet. Spring was a perfect time to live in Sinaloa, and he relished the season with the joy of an alcoholic with a full bottle. His morning shift of bodyguards was dutifully waiting outside for him, two of them on All Terrain Vehicles, with their weapons cradled in their laps, ready for the jog at whatever time it would begin.

"*Hola, chicos.* You up for another good one?" Manuel greeted his men.

No reply answered him. None was expected. These weren't his friends, no matter how warm and fuzzy the *Don* acted, and they understood their role was to protect him, not chat with him.

Sadie whined and nudged his hand with her nose, anxious to get underway. Manuel began stretching, using the columns of his porch for support, smiling at his beloved dog – barely more than a puppy.

Searing lances of white hot pain shot through his upper-body as his chest exploded. Blood splattered Sadie and his men as the burst of gunfire from the brush pounded into his torso. The men froze momentarily before taking cover wherever they could, shooting haphazardly at the area where the gunfire had come from. The two on ATVs gunned their motors and went tearing off in the direction of the sniper, until first one and then the other's head exploded, the vehicles slowing and turning aimlessly now that their operators were dead. The two guards by the porch had taken refuge behind the heavy stone columns, firing without conviction into the dense foliage at the property's perimeter.

Manuel stared blearily up at the complex herringbone pattern of the brickwork in the dome built into the roof over his porch, the *cupula*, his breath gurgling from the holes in his chest as his life ran out onto the rustic stone floor. Sadie approached and nosed his face with her own, licking the flecks of blood from his chin in an effort to comfort him, her warm tongue the last thing he would ever register. His eyes met hers for an instant and then grew wide as he noisily exhaled a long groaning rattle before shuddering into stillness.

Sadie lay beside her master, then stood and circled him. She nudged him again with her nose, and then, as dogs had done since the time they'd joined humans as companions in caves, she sat and pointed her head to the heavens and let forth a baleful howl, filled with all the sadness and pain of the world.

Her beloved master was gone. She was now alone, as only the surviving can be.

CHAPTER 10

"What do you mean Altamar is missing? What the fuck does that mean? Missing?" Jorge Encarlo screamed into his cell phone. "Does that mean he decided to disappear and bang a fifteen year old for a few days, or does that mean he's mulch in a tomato field?"

"*Jefe*, I'm telling you everything I know. I heard from a friend of a friend that he went missing yesterday and his organization is scrambling to find him. Doesn't sound like young love to me…," the voice on the phone advised.

Encarlo was a bulldog of a man, heavily muscled with a buzz cut and a closely cropped four day shadow. "Is there anything else? God damn it, get some more information. I don't care what you have to do. This could be really big if someone's taken the cocksucker out," Encarlo snarled.

"I know. I'm on it. But you know how this goes. Nobody's going to talk if they think they could wind up beheaded for doing so."

"Right. I get it. The problem is that if Altamar's been taken out, we need to move rapidly – or we'll all be as good as dead," Encarlo warned.

"I'm doing everything I can. Really. Give me some more time and I'll find out more. This just came in, and it's not easy getting anyone on his crew to talk. They're not chatty types, if you remember."

Encarlo silently counted to three. "Look. I'm not paying you to *tell* me how hard it is to do your job. I'm paying for you to *do* it. So do your fucking job and get me some intelligence, or I'll find someone who can." Encarlo was fuming and had nobody to take his anger out on. He stared at his little Motorola flip phone, the latest model, and snapped it closed in frustration.

What the hell was going on with Altamar? If he was really missing in a way that suggested he would never be reappearing except as pieces floating in the river, then Encarlo needed to get positioned to take action against the other lieutenants. That was how it worked. If the king was dead, long live whoever was left once the smoke cleared and they hosed the blood off the sidewalks. He didn't make the rules, but he was a survivor, nonetheless. At thirty-one, he was already reputed to be a mover and, even by cartel standards, was utterly ruthless. He'd learned early that shock and awe went a long way towards moving you up the food chain, and so he was prone to violent outbursts of slaughter at the slightest provocation. That was his modus operandi and it had served him in good stead.

Encarlo owned a recycling plant that shipped its product to the United States once it was processed, which had provided excellent cover for shipping other items north as well. His operation was one of many responsible for the growing methamphetamine traffic that was slowly displacing crack cocaine in many areas of the U.S. It was a booming market with a rock-bottom production cost, so the profits from trafficking in the synthetic drug were swelling his accounts. It made the cocaine trade seem like small potatoes, if the growth curve kept up.

He picked unconsciously at a scabbed area above his left ear. It was a nervous tick, one of many he'd developed from the constant pressure to stay one step ahead of the rest of the wolf pack. Encarlo used his own products and consumed a fair amount of both meth and cocaine in a cocktail of stimulants that enabled him to sleep only four hours at a stint. He firmly believed that much of his success was thanks to the long hours he worked, in addition to an innate cunning born of the streets. Those traits, combined with a relentless sadistic bent and a sociopathic streak that would have been the envy of any serial killer, made him the perfect mid-level cartel functionary. His men and his competitors were terrified of him, for good reason – the chemical supplementation often resulted in erratic mood swings; he could be set off on a bloody tirade by virtually anything.

Right now, his antennae were picking up the vibrations of opportunity from the early news of Altamar's mysterious disappearance. He knew that if he could confirm that the man was actually gone for good, he'd be perfectly positioned to capitalize on the situation and take out his rivals before they knew what had hit them. It only got dangerous if all facts were known by all the lieutenants at the same time – that's where it became a killing field until only one was left standing. He'd gone through that multiple times and there was never any guarantee that you would make it through the next one, no matter how much of a badass you were.

The idea of creating a loose coalition like Altamar had never entered his head. Why would he look to his weaker competitors for cooperation when he could simply eliminate them and claim their networks for his own? The outreach approach had worked for Altamar, but in Encarlo's opinion it was the flawed plan of a weak man, which would be evidenced by his having been taken out after only two years at the top of his little hub.

He needed to know what was going on, and he needed to know now. The anxiety was building and he knew from harsh experience that he had to do something salient. Anything. Sitting waiting for feedback was too reactive for his tastes.

Restless, he tapped out a line of cocaine to help him focus, and quickly snorted it using a gold tube he carried for the purpose. He brushed a little on his gums, and shook his head, as if to clear it.

The drug now coursing through his system, Encarlo resolved to see if he could shake loose some information himself. He'd hit the street and see if anything came back from his personal contacts. He had confidence in his men but he couldn't just sit still and wait. Glancing at his watch, he noted that it was already nine-thirty in the morning. Time to move. He stabbed at the keypad of his office phone and barked orders into it, calling for his car to be brought around. He next dialed his second in command and told him to get three men, packing heavy heat, to meet him at his vehicle in five minutes. Encarlo opened his file cabinet, retrieved a Glock 26 9mm pistol and slipped it into his windbreaker pocket. It was a small gun but packed a decent wallop, and he hated having to wear a shoulder holster like some undercover cop. He'd tried an ankle holster, but it had bothered him; it was easier to carry the thing in his pocket.

Encarlo made his way downstairs to the ground level and strode through the office doors, past the heavy industrial equipment in the yard, toward his truck – a silver fully loaded Lincoln Navigator with custom rims and steel armored plates welded into each of the four doors. Three men joined him, all toting a variety of submachine guns. He didn't like to screw around when he went out on the town, and believed in being prepared for an assault at all times. It wasn't so much paranoia as occupational hazard, and it had kept him alive so far. His driver nodded at him as he climbed into the passenger seat, the three enforcers climbing in behind him. One of the reasons he liked the big SUV was because it had enough room for three grown men in the back.

The truck moved toward the front gates, which opened via a configuration of hydraulic pistons activated by the security guard in a booth by the street, and then exploded in a blossom of orange fire. The concussion from the plastique affixed to the gas tank shattered the windows in the nearby buildings as pieces of the truck spiraled through the mushroom cloud of black smoke above it, before inevitably dropping like Icarus back to earth. Nothing survived that sort of a blast, and the men that came running did so with slim hope of salvaging anything.

El Rey took several snapshots with his little camera from across the thoroughfare. He put the Ford Lobo into gear and pulled away down the road to his final destination for the day — the third target, who at this point was already as good as neutralized.

❧≈❦

The lushly green acreage around the Luis Barragan-inspired mansion in the hills outside Culiacan was still in the late morning doldrums, the absence of breeze a seasonal effect that made being outdoors in the swelter unpleasant even for the most seasoned natives. Armed sentries prowled the immaculately manicured grounds around the house, jittery from adrenaline and sweating from the heat. Since early morning they'd been on guard, in a state of high alert.

Ricardo Pilar sat with his inner circle at a square mesquite table in his dining room. The five men who were his closest counselors had serious demeanors, and the air was thick with cigarette smoke and anxiety. He'd gotten several frantic phone calls alerting him about the explosion at Encarlo's plant, and he was troubled by the implications. Pilar sensed that a move was being made, but he wasn't sure who was behind it, and he'd dispatched a group of armed men to see what information they could get from the network of lower-level cartel soldiers that acted as the informal communication channel on the street.

The preliminary reports that had come back weren't good. Two of his four rivals had departed the earth that morning under violent circumstances. There could only be one explanation, and it warranted swift and decisive action. Pilar's nemesis, Valiente, was making a play for the leadership position that Altamar had held, now that the cartel underboss had been officially missing for a significant enough time. That could only mean war to Pilar, a seasoned veteran of countless purges and fights.

Pilar was educated, having attended the university in Monterey, and held a degree in business administration that had served him well when creating and managing his network. He'd studied and taken to heart the lessons of business school, and fancied himself to be superior to the ignorant thugs who'd ascended to equal footing through sheer brutality and the barrel of a gun. While he understood the place for bloodshed, he liked to think of himself as above knee-jerk reactions involving indiscriminate slaughter. But he was no fool, and he sensed that it was time to put down the diploma and strap on the pistols.

His captain, Eduardo, was arguing passionately, and his lieutenants were nodding approval.

"This is our chance. We've been patient, but it's foolishness to sit here waiting for the war to come to us. If Valiente is on the offensive, our best chance to avoid a bloodbath is to make a pre-emptive strike. Cut the head off the snake, and the body stops moving."

Pilar considered the counsel, and then nodded.

"I agree with Eduardo. The explosion that killed Encarlo, when combined with news of Remarosa's execution, is ominous. I have a bad feeling, and I think it's safe to conclude that Valiente is making a major offensive, which would mean we are next. But it's not like we can just waltz in and start shooting to solve the problem. Valiente is far too smart to be taken that way." Pilar pushed back from the table, stood, and began pacing compulsively while he spoke. "While I sympathize with everyone's passion, I'd argue that it's misplaced. Yes, we need to act, but we also need a coherent plan. Right now, all we have is bluster and talk. Let's finish with the discussion about whether removing Valiente is a good idea. It is. Now I want to hear some ideas about how we do so," Pilar said, gesturing with his bottle of Pelgrino to emphasize his point.

His men looked at him, none daring to advance an idea that he would shoot down.

"Here's what we are going to do. I want you to talk among yourselves and think through how best to eliminate Valiente by the end of the day. Then we can put the proposals on the table, and come up with something that makes sense. But don't waste your time arguing for something that's decided. I need ideas, not passion. And my instinct says that we're running out of time, so it's time to get busy." Pilar glanced at his watch and sighed. "I have some commitments I need to attend to. But make no mistake, Valiente must die before the sun goes down, and I am relying on you to come up with how we achieve that." Pilar fixed each man in turn with an intense stare that bristled with quiet menace. He may have had a veneer of civility from his education, but he was as dangerous as a cornered pit viper, and his men were quick to remember how he'd made it to the top of his group. "I'll be back shortly. Make good use of your time."

Pilar strode from the room, shaking his head. This was a classic turf battle, and he needed to get on top of it before Valiente's goons showed up with machine guns. He wasn't afraid of that – his compound was well equipped with all the latest alarms, electronic sensors and advance warning devices, and he had enough firepower to stop a battalion. He felt safe at his home, and he was confident that if an attempt against him was going to be made, it wouldn't happen there. The dense foliage that extended for miles created a natural barrier, and there was only one road in. So for the moment, at least, he was safe.

Pilar had thought through Valiente's likely next step, and he wasn't overly concerned about a frontal assault. But he was vulnerable in ways besides the obvious. If this power struggle lasted very long, business would be negatively impacted, and that would cause disruption among the lieutenants, which could be as dangerous as a shooting war. It was bad enough that Pilar's rivals were homicidal psychopaths without him having to worry about younger, more junior aspirants to the throne cutting his heart out while he slept.

He moved to the pocket doors that separated the great room from the rear deck and took in the beauty of his grounds. It was times of extreme adversity that defined leaders, and even though he fancied himself a civilized man, he understood that it was necessary to be swift an unequivocal in his response to this threat. Pilar had no problem killing – it went with the territory. But he'd always tried to keep the violence at arm's length, which while not always successful, enabled him to maintain his presumption of superiority.

Something in the tree line caught the sun, and Pilar squinted to make it out. The hair on his arms bristled as he detected movement and a flash, and the neurons in his brain were ordering his body to drop to the floor as the high-velocity partially jacketed round blew his cheekbone apart, taking the better part of his cerebrum with it. By the time the guards had a chance to respond to the single shot from the perimeter, the shooter had long since departed, the sound of the dirt bike he'd pushed silently for a half mile a noisy memory in the woods.

৵৽৻

Mexico City's sky was laden with hulking, dark clouds when *El Rey* pulled over the hills and into the infamously dangerous metropolitan traffic. The Toyota had run like a champ, was a pleasure to drive, softening the blows of the rutted patches between Culiacan and DF, or *Distrito Federal*, as the locals referred to Mexico City. He'd gotten the contact information of a man Valiente, his new patron and sponsor, had known since childhood. Valiente had made a phone call and proposed a relationship that his friend couldn't possibly refuse. The man owned a pawn shop but he'd fallen into leveraging his contacts in the underworld and being a facilitator for extermination work – the human kind. It was a difficult role for him because he was basically a good and decent man, but the money was simply too attractive to turn down for a no-risk proposition. He had three contractors who handled domestic disputes and business disagreements, and he took twenty percent of the contract price to handle the money and vet the clients.

El Rey needed someone trustworthy to launder his money and deal with the payments. If he was going to do this professionally, he needed a front office, so to speak – and professional representation. He could handle sourcing the jobs but he couldn't haul around several million dollars in hundreds and be effective. He needed a banker and an accountant. Valiente's contact seemed ideally suited for the role. And Valiente had warned his friend what he was dealing with, lest he get the bright idea to take *El Rey*'s money and run for the hills. In the cartels, if you vouched for someone and made an introduction, and then that someone screwed the person you'd introduced, you could expect to be held accountable for your recommendation's actions. Valiente had seen more than enough of *El Rey*'s handiwork in a short period to know he didn't want that coming after him.

The *narcotraficante* chief had become *El Rey*'s biggest admirer and had promised to spread the word of his prowess in return for a commitment to never accept a contract on him. That seemed reasonable to *El Rey*, and Valiente was an up-and-comer in the most powerful cartel on the planet, so as sponsors go, he could do worse. His plan was to limit his activity to a few hits a year, but to steadily increase the fee he charged as well as the level of difficulty of the sanctions he accepted until he became the highest paid killer in the world. Mexico was the right place for that, given the amount of money flowing through the cartels, although he'd heard good things about Russia, too. Problem there was that he didn't speak the language. He'd studied English in school and, of course, there was his Spanish. But that was it. So he wouldn't be doing any work in St. Petersburg or Vladivostok.

He merged toward the right lane and took an off ramp from the clogged freeway into an even more congested area of the city. After circling around for half an hour, he eventually located the pawn shop and managed to find a parking spot. He threw his black duffel bag over his shoulder and made his way two blocks to the store. The neighborhood was sketchy even by Mexico City standards, which was saying a lot, but then again, money lenders of last resort didn't tend to be located in the ritziest areas.

At the glass door to the shop, he noted bars everywhere, providing security against night incursions, as well as a roll-up metal awning that would completely seal off the storefront. With all the bars it seemed like overkill, but *El Rey* liked that – it hinted at a man who took precautions, and who over-engineered them. That was a careful man, which is what he needed. The establishment itself was modest by any measure, which suggested a lack of braggadocio or hubris. Again, strongly positive from *El Rey*'s position.

He pushed open the entry door and walked into a small, somewhat shabby showroom with a few inexpensive glass cases showcasing the tarnished treasures of the impoverished and downtrodden. Silver infant cups, cheap watches, scarred gold chains, obsolete cameras. *El Rey* was liking this guy's style more and more. This was the last place in the world he would expect to find a man who handled the affairs of high-end contract killers. Nothing about the shop spoke of money or success or high-rolling, which were usually hand in hand with cartel-related businesses. This just said boring.

El Rey liked boring.

He approached the barred window, which was fabricated out of inch-thick bullet-proof glass, and pushed the button next to it, listening as the buzzer echoed in the rear, behind the heavy steel door to his right. He studied the door: it was built like a bank's, although it was probably heavier by the looks of the four massive hinge plates welded in place. He rapped a knuckle against the wall next to it – at least foot-thick reinforced concrete. A meager enterprise with security like a vault. Interesting.

Footsteps approached, and then a small man with a beret and a graying goatee appeared at the window.

"Yes?" he asked by way of greeting.

"I'm here for an eleven o'clock meeting," *El Rey* said.

"Ah. Of course." The steel door buzzed and *El Rey* rushed to grab the handle before it stopped. He swung it open and noted that he'd been correct. The steel slab was very heavy indeed, and the locking mechanism was industrial grade.

"Nice door."

"Mmmm. Two one-inch steel plates with a titanium core. Custom made in Austria. Cost a bit, but worth it," the little man said. He extended his hand. "Jaime Tortora, at your service. Please. Come back to my offices. Would you like anything to drink? Water? Coffee? Beer?"

El Rey shook his hand. "No, thank you. I don't drink coffee or alcohol. I'll follow you."

Tortora walked down the dimly lit hallway and opened the door of his office. The two men entered and Tortora gestured to one of the chairs in front of his desk. He took his seat behind it and leaned forward, both hands on the surface, visible at all times. *El Rey* noticed this reassuring stance, and nodded almost imperceptibly as he sat, placing the duffle on the chair next to him.

"A mutual friend of some distinction called and indicated there was an opportunity for us to help each other," Tortora began, then hesitated. "You may speak freely. I have eavesdropping detection equipment in place, and if you were wired, I'd know. I also sweep the office once a week. Vocational paranoia, you could say."

El Rey fixed him with a tranquil gaze. "I am looking for someone who can help me; act as a back office and clearing system for my payments and due diligence on clients," *El Rey* said.

"Ah, yes. Well, that's what I do. I take twenty percent if I source the clients, or ten percent if you do. I can deal with cash, although that's an additional ten percent right off the top for the bank to handle. I prefer wire transfers or bearer instruments, and have an extensive infrastructure to accommodate those. Austria and the Caymans, with a second set of accounts in Panama and Lichtenstein. All owned by dummy front companies out of Hong Kong or Latvia." Tortora reached over and took a sip of water from a glass near his computer monitor. "I can assist in setting up a structure for you, if that is necessary. My only advice if you intend to do so yourself is to hire a professional. The money trail is often the weak link."

"I'd be interested in having you set up a mechanism. I want money to wind up in Uruguay or Belize. I've read about setting up companies there, International Business Companies, where the ownership can be held via bearer shares, which are untraceable," *El Rey* observed.

"Yes, but there are some problems with that. I'd advise a more involved structure, where we first create a trust whose beneficiary is a Swiss corporation, and then have the trust's attorney set up the IBC and the bank account. Do you need papers? Passports? Identity documents of any kind?" Tortora asked.

"Now that you mention it, yes. I'll need a Spanish passport, a Mexican birth certificate and passport, and a third passport, maybe from El Salvador or Peru. I'd like them all in different names and, if possible, legitimately issued – not forgeries."

"That can be done. But it will be expensive. Probably a couple of hundred thousand dollars. It would be way cheaper to have high quality forgeries created," Tortora advised, glancing at the young man. "But fakes are not as bullet-proof, no pun intended."

"The money isn't a concern. How long will it take?"

"For legitimate documents? A month or two. I can get the Mexican paperwork faster, so if you have pressing travel plans, figure two weeks for that. The rest are more complicated," Tortora explained.

"All right. Get the Mexican one as soon as possible. Now let's talk about how this will work. I have a large sum of cash I need washed so it can be transferred into a bank account once you have the structure set up. Why the ten percent for cash?"

"That's what I have to pay to circumvent the anti-money laundering laws at the bank. It's the going rate. How much cash are we talking, anyway?" Tortora asked.

"Two million dollars, *mas o menos*. And likely two hundred fifty thousand per job, couple of times a year. To start."

Tortora didn't blink. "I can handle that. Do you have any questions for me?"

"How many other contractors do you handle?"

"Three. But smaller scale than what you're doing. Fifty grand here and there."

"I'd like you to drop them. How much would I need to bring in to replace their income?" *El Rey* asked.

"Depends. Will you be sourcing your own clients?"

"Absolutely. All you'll be doing is handling the money. I'll even collect it most of the time, unless there's a wire transfer, which is doubtful, given my clientele."

Tortora considered the question carefully.

"One of the issues is that if you're killed, I have lost my business and will have to start over." Tortora said, then quickly punched some numbers into his desktop calculator.

"I'm not planning on getting killed."

"Nobody does. But it's a risk that needs to be adjusted for. I think that if we went fifteen percent up to the first million of income per year, then ten for anything above, I could cut my other contractors loose. But I'd need to see at least half a million gross per year of income to make it worth my while. That's a lot of contracts," Tortora said.

"Not to brag, but soon that will only be two contracts a year, and then only one. So not that many." The assassin sat back and studied Tortora's face. "I accept your proposal. Fifteen of the first million, ten above that. Bank fees to come off the top, pre-split." He lifted the duffel and placed it on the desk. "This is two million five hundred thousand dollars. Take the paperwork money and the fees to create the structure out of it. What will the structuring run, anyway?" *El Rey* asked.

"Not that much. Maybe fifty by the time everything's set up. Fifteen for the company formations, and the rest for lubrication and consultants and attorneys. Then maybe ten grand a year thereafter for filing fees."

"Okay. So call it two point two million cash after deducting for that. Minus ten percent for the banks, leaves us at an even two. I'll give you fifty of that for your time, given that you haven't done any heavy lifting beyond opening some accounts. Cut your other operators loose within six months. By then, I'll be back and working," *El Rey* instructed.

"Do you have any questions of me? Guarantees about the safety of your money?"

"Our mutual friend must have explained a little. I know you have an apartment upstairs and a home, with a daughter in university. I know everything about you. I can find you wherever you are, no matter how deep you think you've gone, so, no, I'm not too worried. Then again, you'd be stupid to try it, because over the next few years you'll make a lot of money as my fee increases. And it will. I'm already at two hundred grand a hit, and that will move to two-fifty on the next ones." *El Rey* wasn't bragging or threatening. His calm, soft voice was merely stating fact.

Tortora appraised him anew.

"I believe you. My friend indicated that you'd done the impossible in no time. And he's not an easy man to impress. If he's singing your praises, you'll have your hands full with work whenever you want it."

They discussed more details, such as names for the passports and logistics of contacting each other, and after an hour, concluded their meeting.

El Rey liked the little man. He was perfect. Avaricious but old enough so he wouldn't be a runner. Morally neutral on the issue of the business, and not squeamish. A good combination. The money would all accumulate in accounts only *El Rey* had signature authority over, using his new passports and names, so it would be in no danger once it hit his banks. As to the cash, he wasn't worried about that disappearing. There were some things that just weren't worth doing, and he got the sense that the pawn shop proprietor had quickly figured out that fucking him over was one of them.

He had a spring in his step as he returned to his Toyota, one more problem dealt with. This was shaping up nicely, perfectly following the plan he'd had in mind since he was seventeen. He would become the highest paid assassin in the world within a few years, famous for meticulously planned sanctions that defied belief. He would become a sort of miracle worker. *El Rey* would be a name that cartel bosses used to frighten their kids at night, and it would be synonymous with a ghost, a phantom who could do the impossible. In a world where nobody got scared, an environment where violence and death was daily currency, there would be something that even the most hardened veterans would fear.

The name of the beast.

El Rey.

CHAPTER 11

The jungle was everywhere. That was *El Rey*'s impression of Costa Rica, if anyone were to ask him. It was everything he'd always imagined when he heard the term rain forest, right down to the toucans and monkeys. And even though everyone spoke Spanish it was as different from Mexico as he imagined South America would be.

He had arrived in the tiny Central American country to learn how to fly. Specifically, how to operate prop planes and helicopters, should he ever need to be able to do so. Rather than resting on his laurels, he'd made a personal commitment to continually learn new skills, expanding his abilities as well as the likelihood of survival. In the end, he hadn't been able to convince the Mexican special forces to teach him how to operate a plane, so the first stop after he'd gotten his new papers was to find a place off the beaten path where he could master the discipline. And Costa Rica was well off any radar – while it had a decent amount of infrastructure, even by Mexican standards it was backwards, as were its neighbors, Nicaragua, El Salvador and Honduras. He'd considered each of those in turn, but decided on Costa Rica after researching the alternatives –

the others were too unstable, with a considerable cartel presence he would rather avoid unless working.

The flight school in the capital city of San Jose had been more than willing to teach him everything he wanted to know for certification of fixed wing, and he had clocked almost all the required hours he needed. Helicopters were a different story, but he'd been able to find a pilot who was willing to unofficially give him lessons and explain everything about the mechanics of the crafts. *El Rey* had now been in Costa Rica for three months and was about ready to get the hell out and back to what he considered civilization. For his money, San Jose couldn't hold a candle to Guadalajara or Monterrey or Mexico City, but it has served its purpose. One thing he was sure of was that he wouldn't likely be back unless he lost a bet.

He pulled up to the hangar at the edge of the runway and got out of his rental car, and after greeting his flight trainer, they moved to the small Cessna 172 prop plane to undertake their pre-flight checklist. *El Rey* was now certified, but he wanted to clock as many hours as possible while he was in Central America so he was completely confident in his abilities.

Just as they were getting into the cockpit, his cell phone rang, and he excused himself for a moment and took a call.

It was Tortora.

"Our friend called me. He has an urgent matter for you. Thinks it could be a real opportunity. How soon can you be in Sinaloa?" Tortora asked.

El Rey considered the question, eyeing the surrounding airport as he did so. "Tomorrow, at the latest. I have to look at flight schedules. Worst case I can charter a plane.

I'll check in later to let you know what my timing looks like. Did he indicate how urgent?"

"He didn't go into detail. Said he'd prefer to discuss it with you in person. Shall I tell him you're en route?" Tortora asked.

"Please. But don't tell him from where. That's our little secret."

"Of course not. Call me when you know more," Tortora said, and then the line went dead.

El Rey returned to the little plane.

"Sorry, Roger, got to cut out. Tell me. Just for the sake of conversation – how much would it cost to hire a plane to get me to Mexico City if I needed to leave in the next few hours? My mother isn't well," *El Rey* explained.

"I'm sorry to hear that. What's the distance? Fifteen hundred miles?"

"A little less. More like twelve hundred."

"Boy. I don't know. You want me to make some calls and find out? Not too many prop planes could make that without setting down at least once. You care if it's a jet or prop?"

"Not really. But I need to get going by one o'clock on the outside." *El Rey* checked his watch. It was nine in the morning.

"I know a guy who has that King Air over there. He might be into it. But it would probably be ten to fifteen grand…"

"Make the call."

An hour later, and they'd gotten nowhere, so *El Rey* went to the passenger terminal and checked with Taca. They had a five o'clock flight that would get him into Mexico City a couple of hours later, and then he could get a plane to Culiacan in the morning. He booked it, paying in cash, and returned to his leased condo to pack. He didn't have much – a rucksack with his clothes, thirty thousand dollars in hundreds, and a credit card in the name of one of his companies, with a fifty grand limit. In his line of work, he'd found it paid to travel light.

He set his bag by the door and then retrieved a rag and a bottle of ammonia-based cleaner, and began the tedious but necessary process of wiping down every area he might have touched. The cleanup took an hour and a half, but he had time to kill, and nobody had ever gotten caught by being overly careful. When he was done, he took a final look around the small condo and nodded, then wiped down the doorknob and deadbolt, twisting it open using the rag, and then repeated the process after closing it. He sauntered down the stairs to the front foyer and eased the steel and glass entry door open, then dropped the rag into a scarred garbage can at the end of the block.

The flight to Mexico City was tiresome, and once he landed he exhaled a sigh of relief. For all its exotic charms, Costa Rica hadn't been his cup of tea and he was glad to be back on home turf. He checked the flight schedules to Culiacan and found one that departed at eight a.m., which would put him in Culiacan with time to spare for an afternoon meeting with Valiente. He booked a room at one of the large hotels connected to the airport terminal that catered to business travelers and settled in for the night, preferring to order room service than venture into town.

The next day, he touched down in Culiacan and rented a car at the airport. Now that he had a variety of IDs it made life much easier. He could change around who he was whenever he felt the urge, avoiding any chance of there being a pattern in his coming and going. An admittedly expensive set of precautions, but ultimately worth it to him.

When he arrived at Valiente's office, the cartel honcho greeted him warmly and invited him to sit. After some cursory pleasantries were dispensed with, including *El Rey*'s congratulations on Valiente becoming the new regional chief for the Sinaloa cartel's northern operations – Altamar's former role – they got down to business.

Valiente slid a grainy black and white photograph of a swarthy man across his desk to *El Rey*, who studied it before looking up at the *narcotraficante*, his face devoid of expression.

"That's German Coriente. Known as '*El Chilango*'. He used to be one of the ranking members of the Jalisco Cartel," Valiente explained.

El Rey waited patiently for more.

"He disappeared a year ago, after a contract was put out on him by the head of our Sinaloa cartel, *Don* Aranas. The contractor who took the assignment failed to execute him and was never heard from again. We assume that *El Chilango* stopped him somehow, and extracted information from him on who hired him to do the hit. Shortly afterwards, *El Chilango* disappeared, and it has taken a full year for us to find him," Valiente continued.

"Where is he?"

"Australia. He got a Chilean passport and moved to Sydney, where nobody knows him. He's hired several mercenaries for security, and bought a wine exportation company to establish residence there."

El Rey nodded. "Sounds like he got as far away from Mexico as you can get, and he's out of the game. So why go after him? Not to talk myself out of work, but rather so I understand the motivation," *El Rey* said.

"What do you care why? We offer a contract, you take it. That's how it works, no?"

El Rey held Valiente's gaze and shook his head. "If I need to fly halfway around the world to kill someone, I need to know everything. That's one of my conditions. Otherwise, respectfully, hire someone else. Although it sounds like your last experience with a contractor on this guy didn't work out so well. So again, tell me, why go after a player who's taken himself off the table and is living on the other end of the planet?" *El Rey* asked.

Valiente initially looked annoyed, but then remembered who he was talking to. *El Rey* was a dangerous man, even by cartel standards. Not someone you wanted to make an enemy of.

"It's personal. The hit is personal. Unfinished business."

"Personal? With Aranas? What could *El Chilango* have possibly done to bring that upon himself?" Now *El Rey* was genuinely curious.

"It's a long story. Apparently, the two men knew each other from many years ago and then when Sinaloa went to war with the Jalisco cartel, things escalated out of control. That was almost a decade ago, and it went on for years, with heavy casualties on both sides."

"They're still enemies to this day, no?" *El Rey* asked.

"Yes. And they'll always be enemies. Too much blood spilled to ever build bridges. What happened was that, during the worst of the war, *El Chilango* sent an execution team to take out Aranas. But they botched it. You can probably guess how that went down. Four killers from Veracruz with AK-47s – playing cowboys. Anyway, turns out Aranas wasn't where they were told he would be, so when they shot up the car he was supposed to be traveling in, it wasn't him. It was his twelve year old daughter, Imelda, on her way to ballet class." Valiente paused to allow that to sink in. "She was apparently a rare talent. And beautiful. They tell me she lived for almost a month on machines before the injuries were too much for her. So it's personal. Every day *El Chilango* breathes is an affront to Aranas, and he wants the man erased. Which brings us to why you are here, gracing our town with your presence."

The assassin nodded. "What are the details?"

"The most important thing to understand is that Aranas doesn't just want a hit. He wants *El Chilango* to suffer. A lot. I had mentioned to him how adept you've been in handling our transactions, and he authorized me to reach out to you. So here I am. And now, here are you as well."

"What's the contract price?" *El Rey* was curious how badly they wanted him dead.

"Two hundred fifty thousand dollars."

El Rey shook his head, holding Valiente's gaze. "Too low for the risk involved. A foreign country, likely many unusual expenses, a police force that can't be bought, foreign mercenaries...I don't mean to sound like an ingrate, but that won't cover it," *El Rey* explained.

Valiente sat back, exasperated. "Then what's the right number for you to take this on? I know I can get any of a dozen men who would jump at doing this for fifty."

"You tried that once. These aren't the kinds of situation where you look to save money. If you want the best and you want a guaranteed result, you will pay more than hiring someone who will try, and fail. Sounds like if you blow it one more time, he'll disappear on you for good. I'm not sure I'd want to have to deliver that news to *Don* Aranas." *El Rey* studied a point on the wall for a few moments. "My number is three hundred thousand."

"Done."

"Plus expenses, which will probably come to another fifty to a hundred. I won't know until I get over there and see the lay of the land."

Valiente's eyes narrowed to slits. "Fair enough."

"And I'll need specialized gear once I'm in-country, so you'll have to find a local who can get hard-to-find items for me. I won't know what they are until I'm on the ground, but it could be specialized weapons, or explosives, or gas. Don't know. Do you have any contacts there?" *El Rey* asked.

"There's nowhere in the world we don't have contacts. I'll find someone." Valiente smiled. "Is there anything else?"

"I expect you to pay for the travel, too. I'll bet first class tickets to Sydney aren't going to be cheap." *El Rey* rose to his feet. "I can leave tomorrow. I'll need half the money in advance, as usual, and an ATM card set up so I can withdraw up to a hundred thousand dollars on it from anywhere in the world. That way I can pull money out as necessary." El Rey paused, thinking. "No, better yet, give me fifty in cash, and fifty on an ATM. Do you have a package on him?"

Valiente pushed a manila envelope across the table. *El Rey* opened the top, glanced at the contents and nodded. Valiente reached below his desk and retrieved a slim briefcase.

"Here's two hundred and fifty, cash. Call that two for you, and fifty for expenses. I'll have a card for you within a few days and will send it to you by DHL. That way you'll have it within a week, on the outside. My guess is you'll want to spend some time lining things up before you do this. Am I right?"

El Rey ignored the question. "So you would have paid five hundred?"

"We think very highly of your talents. But it sounds like you'll wind up costing four by the time this is done, so you can make it up on the next one. And if you pull this off for Aranas, there will be as many next ones as you want." Valiente grinned. "It's only money, right?"

"You have a point. I'll look into hotels and flights. Timeframe for the hit?"

"If you can bring it in within ten days that will do."

"Shouldn't be an issue, if he's only got a couple of bodyguards. Do you have dossiers on them?" *El Rey* asked.

"It's in there. One's South African, the other British — who saw a tour in Afghanistan. Not pushovers, that's for sure."

"They all die the same."

"Too true. You need anything else from my end?"

"Just get in touch with someone who can get me whatever I need in Australia. I'll get a cell phone once I'm there and touch base for the contact info." *El Rey* stood, and hefted the briefcase. "Hate to leave a hundred on the table, but it is what it is."

"I have a feeling if you make it ugly enough for *El Chilango*, there's a chance of a bonus. Aranas isn't that price sensitive."

"Tell me. Does he have any other children?" *El Rey* asked.

Valiente looked at him strangely. "I think he's got two sons. I'm not sure, though. We aren't that close," Valiente admitted.

"His only daughter. No, I imagine he's not price sensitive at all." He held up the briefcase and moved towards the door, hesitating before he left. When he turned to face Valiente a final time, even the hardened cartel drug lord's stomach lurched when *El Rey* offered a diminutive smirk.

"I'll get creative."

CHAPTER 12

Sydney was unlike any place *El Rey* had ever been. From the time he got off the plane, his Qantas first class experience a welcome luxury on the fifteen hour flight from Los Angeles, he was struck by how clean everything was. It was as if someone had scrubbed every surface right before he got there – but the entire town, as far as he could see wandering around the downtown area, was like that.

He took a cab from the airport to his hotel a few blocks from Sydney harbor and stowed his gear, locking his cash in the hotel room safe and unpacking his hygiene kit. After a few hours of sleep to get adjusted to the seven hour time difference, he set out to explore the town so he'd understand the layout. A four minute walk to the ferry terminal at Circular Quay quickly convinced him that the town was filled with tourists, so one more from Mexico wouldn't stick out, which had been one of his fears. He never wanted to be memorable anywhere he went but there would be no such problem here – judging by the host of accents and languages he heard as he moved along the waterfront from the quaint shopping area called 'The Rocks' toward the opera house.

El Rey approached the iconic theater, which sat on a point at the water's edge, its aggressive shape unmistakable from almost every photo and postcard he'd seen. He kept walking towards the ocean and soon found himself in a verdant, well-groomed park, where he passed young lovers reposing on the grass, stealing moments together after school.

The weather was the equivalent of late autumn in Australia, the seasons being reversed from the Northern hemisphere, but it was still relatively mild and sunnier than he'd expected. And so clean. Being used to Mexico, Sydney was a shock to his system in that it was so aseptic. Even as he made his way out of the park into an area that was supposedly seedier, it was as nice as some of the best neighborhoods back home. He stopped at a long pier with a sign out front that announced it as Finger Wharf and looked in at a hotel built over the harbor – the W Sydney – and felt immediately comfortable in the dimly lit, soothing, minimalistic contemporary lobby. It was deserted, save for a young woman working behind the desk and, based on the ambience and the solitary location, he decided right then and there that he'd be moving to the W the following day.

Walking away from the harbor, he explored the area inland from the hotel. It quickly degraded into a run-down industrial district with warehouses alongside shabby lower-income housing. A few of the buildings looked as though they were about to undergo renovation but much of the area was desolate and he found himself the only person on the streets – mid-afternoon on a weekday. He made a mental note: this was perfect for what he had in mind. He'd begun the outlines of a rough plan on the plane, purely conceptual, but if everything panned out it could work well.

After another hour meandering the streets adjacent to the waterfront he made his way back to the hotel, where he hailed a cab and asked the driver to drop him two streets away from the address where *El Chilango* now lived. They drove into an upscale area fifteen minutes from the city center, and the cab stopped in front of a small market a block from the harbor.

The neighborhood was eclectic, exhibiting a hodgepodge of architectural styles coexisting in a dissonant manner. Everything from elegant multi-story turn-of-the-century Victorian mansions to post-modern contemporary could be found. It was certainly a prosperous area, judging by the cars and the trim on the houses. *El Rey* knew that waterfront homes anywhere in the world were always the most expensive – he figured that Australia would be no different. He bought a bottle of water from the bored shopkeeper and then strolled towards the target's address, relieved to find that the sidewalks were empty. When he reached the T junction that dead-ended into the target street he deliberately avoided *El Chilango*'s house, preferring to make a left on the street that ran along the waterfront homes rather than a right. He knew that the former cartel chief's home was four down on the right from the intersection where he made the turn, and he didn't really need to see much more than he did by glancing down the street as though he was a stray sightseer who'd wandered into the area. He knew from the report he'd read on the plane that it was a two story, five bedroom waterfront home on a double lot, with security lighting at night activated by motion sensors on the sides of the house, as well as the street.

Comfortable with the feel of the neighborhood, he walked six blocks until he came to a major artery, and had a coffee shop call him a taxi while he enjoyed a cup of pungent green tea. Once back at his hotel, he did a quick calculation of the time back home before going downstairs to ask the concierge where he could get a cell phone. The pert young woman directed him four blocks away, and soon he was paying for the latest model Nokia with a three month prepaid service plan. As soon as it was activated, he fished a matchbook out of his pocket and dialed the country code and phone number he'd jotted down. Valiente's voice answered.

"I'm here. Do you have anything for me on a local contact?" *El Rey* asked.

Valiente gave him a Sydney cell number.

"You'll want to ask for Victor," Valiente said, then terminated the call, there being nothing more to discuss.

He did as instructed, and a gravelly, Australian voice answered. *El Rey* told the man he was from out of town, and used Valiente's name by way of entre. They arranged to meet an hour later at a café immediately in front of the ferry terminal. Victor would be wearing an orange T-shirt with a blue windbreaker and tan cargo pants.

El Rey watched from his vantage point across the busy common as a man dressed as described entered the café and sat down by the window. After five minutes of scanning the quay to ensure there was no surveillance, *El Rey* strolled in and took a seat opposite him. Victor was in his mid forties and rail thin, with a heavily lined, sun-damaged face boasting the perennial flush of the habitual hard drinker, spectacularly crooked teeth, and thatches of salt-and-pepper hair pointing in all directions. He looked like nothing so much as an absentminded professor with a boozing problem.

"G'day, mate. Name's Victor. I was told to give yah whatever yah needed, and mum's the word," Victor started. *El Rey* couldn't really make out what the man was saying, so instead began speaking in his quiet, calm voice. His English was passable from years of study, but still heavily accented with Spanish inflection.

"I will need a boat with a captain tomorrow to take me around the harbor so I can look over some places. I have also made a list of items I will require. And I think I've found an area with some industrial space you can rent inexpensively. If not, I need a small warehouse in a quiet neighborhood where it will have no neighbors, good for privacy, yes?" *El Rey* handed him the neatly hand-written note with his requirements.

Victor studied it, and nodded. "No worries, mate. Good as done — but it'll run yah dear. My guess is twenty grand American at least, plus the boat tour. How many rounds you need for the rifle and the pistol?" Victor asked.

"A hundred for the rifle and its magazines, and fifty for the pistol and its spares. Will the night vision equipment be a problem?"

"Mate, none of it's a problem. Just a matter of money. Give me two days and I'll have the whole lot sorted," Victor assured him. "Now in the meantime, what about yerself? Need any company? Interested in the ladies?" Seeing the vacant expression on the assassin's face and intuiting a lack of interest, he tried again. "Or maybe the boys? A little *Cage aux Follees*, if yah catch my meaning? Whatever yer flavor, Victor's the man…"

"Just the items on the list, some warehouse space with no neighbors and a boat with a captain. Nothing fancy. Something that will blend in. I'd like to use it tomorrow for around four hours. And make sure it's got some fishing equipment onboard. I'll call you in the morning. Will that work for you?" *El Rey* asked, ignoring Victor's offer.

Victor assured him that it would, and they quickly parted ways, Victor to procure the necessary hardware and *El Rey* to have an early dinner and get some sleep.

The following day, Victor had made arrangements for a cabin cruiser to pick *El Rey* up at the pier marina that hosted the W Hotel and the adjacent condominiums and restaurants. He checked out of his current hotel and walked over to the W, taking a waterfront room for a week on the third floor. Once he'd unpacked, he grabbed a quick bite downstairs before heading out to meet the boat, a heavy set of binoculars around his neck. It was a thirty-eight-foot Riviera sports fisherman with twin diesel engines, and soon they were cutting through the chop at a fair clip. *El Rey* gave the captain GPS coordinates for the portion of the harbor he wanted to anchor in and fish. The man looked at him as though he was crazy.

"Won't catch much there but muck suckers, mate," he advised.

"That's okay. I just like being on the water, enjoying the scenery and looking at all the beautiful houses," *El Rey* explained.

They motored to the designated spot and dropped anchor. The captain dutifully got out two light-tackle salt water fishing rods and a bag of frozen bait. *El Rey* played along and allowed the man to drop a line into the water for him, then went inside the salon, where the heavily tinted windows blocked anyone from seeing in. He raised his binoculars and scanned the house, noting the neighbors' homes, searching for anything that could afford him an advantage. He paid special attention to the shore area and the distances between the homes, which wasn't much. Fortunately, *El Chilango* had built tall walls on either side for security and privacy, so he wouldn't have to deal with neighbor issues once inside. As they sat there, bobbing in the wake of the boats cruising past them, he noted that there were three security men nosing around, not just the one the report would have led him to believe. So either the house had received some sort of warning, or the surveillance had been sloppy. Instead of a day man and a night one, there were six total: three and three.

They spent two hours at anchor, the boat rocking gently, with *El Rey* mainly watching the house. By lunchtime, he'd seen enough. The target had been visible several times in his living room and bedroom, and it would have been a cinch to take him out with a single shot. Unfortunately, that wasn't what he was being paid to do. Reconciling himself to the unpleasant reality that he'd have to do this the hard way, he announced to the captain that it was time to leave. Just then one of the two rods screamed as line tore off the reel – the skipper ran to tighten the drag. He set the hook and then offered the pole to *El Rey*, who shook his head – he had no interest in trying to fight the fish. After a few moments the line went limp; when the captain reeled it in, the leader had been bitten through.

"Probably a shark," he said.

"Are there a lot of them around here?" *El Rey* asked, curious.

"In the harbor, yah get some sand sharks and a few larger ones. Out in the ocean, there's great whites, ya know. Frightful big buggers. One of em gets ya, yer day's pretty much ruined. Don't want to mess with one of those, I'll tell yah," he warned.

"No. I'd imagine not."

That evening, *El Rey* had a phone discussion with Victor, and they arranged a meeting for the next day to look over the industrial space he'd gotten and inventory the hardware.

In the morning, a blue Ford sedan pulled to the curb by the original hotel *El Rey* had stayed at. Victor grinned from behind the wheel, inviting him to get in. Soon they were motoring to the deserted area near the W, and after a few turns, they arrived at a bleak strip of old industrial warehouses. Victor got out and opened one of the heavy steel doors and they stepped into a dilapidated twenty-by-forty brick space that reeked of stale air and urine. *El Rey* tried the lights – two fluorescent bulbs flickered above as if struggling to stay lit, and then with a flash, suddenly illuminated.

The assassin studied the shabby interior, his arms crossed, and then nodded.

"This will do."

Glancing around the dank room a final time, *El Rey* dictated an additional list of items he'd need, based on his surveillance of the target and his appraisal of his new workspace. Victor scribbled furiously in a small notebook as *El Rey* ticked off the requirements. Finished, they eyed the overhead steel beams that supported the roof, before *El Rey* made two more requests. Victor nodded, and assured him that within forty-eight hours he would have the space outfitted, and then went to the car and removed a long duffle with the requested hardware and brought it inside the space. *El Rey* inspected each item carefully and nodded in approval. Perhaps Victor resembled a buffoon, but he'd gotten everything right on the first try. That was good. He hoped Victor did as well on the second round of stuff. None of it was that specialized, so he was confident the man would be able to get it all.

Three days later, they returned to the warehouse. It had been completely transformed. *El Rey* was impressed. He'd spent parts of the last few days in the target's neighborhood, driving around with Victor, studying the layout, and had a watcher confirm the number of guards at night, as well. *El Chilango* rarely left the house, so whatever his wine business was, you could apparently run it from home. That would make things somewhat harder – it would be far easier to stage something while a target was in transit, but you played the cards you were dealt, and *El Rey* was confident.

Tomorrow would be show time, and he would either justify the considerable money he'd been spending over the course of his antipodean vacation – or die trying.

CHAPTER 13

Stiff gusts of wind blew through the tall oak trees near the water's edge, occasionally eliciting a moaning lament at the air's harmonic passage through the branches. It was a partially cloudy night with only a sliver of a moon peeking through the overcast. The lights from the surrounding homes on the harbor twinkled and danced as the roiling surface of the water reflected them up, moving in time with the swell from the harbor mouth as it surged against the outcropping shore of Point Piper, as the upscale neighborhood was called – a nub of land thrusting into the water, creating Double Bay on one side and Rose Bay on the other.

Three tough-looking guards prowled the grounds of the target's home, two stationed front and back, with one circulating around. It was a lot of security for a relatively modest home in a safe area. The neighbors had to wonder who the occupant was. The men did their best to appear discreet but they were obviously trained killers with military bearings and the tell-tale bulges of handguns under their windbreaker jackets.

This was the easiest duty any of them had ever had. Endless hours of nothing guarding a nobody from imagined threats that never materialized. They'd gotten complacent over the nine months they'd been working the gig, which was understandable given the uneventful nature of the job. But if it made the man happy, it was his money to spend as he liked and they weren't going to complain. For fifteen thousand American dollars a month apiece, they'd put on a trapeze performance or ride unicycles on a tightrope every evening if that's what their patron wanted.

It was quiet at one a.m. on a weeknight, with very few cars winding their way along the New South Head road that tracked the coastline. Sydney's suburbs were asleep, the citizenry enjoying its well-deserved rest in the privileged enclave.

A small black inflatable dinghy moved towards the shore, slicing through the small swells as it made its silent way through the night. A hundred yards off the point, the operator dropped an anchor into the water before cutting the little electric motor. He sat, rising and falling with the waves, getting a sense for the amplitude and acclimating himself.

The waterside of the target's home glimmered through the luminescent green of the night vision scope. *El Rey* could easily make out the sentry, sitting on the rear deck, smoking a cigarette and reading a book. Very unprofessional, but then again, given that the biggest threat the security team thought they were likely to encounter was an enraged koala bear on a eucalyptus-fueled rampage, he could appreciate their lackadaisical attitude. It would be the last mistake any of them ever made. But still, it was understandable.

The crosshairs of the modified M4 assault rifle's night scope bounced up and down from the waves, the weapon made ungainly from the additional weight of the long flash-suppressing silencer affixed to the barrel's end. The surface movement would decrease the likely accuracy, but he'd spent a few hours in a rural area out of town sighting it in with Victor yesterday for exactly the required distance and the margin of error was acceptable – down to a variance of two inches. An additional factor would be the brisk breeze, and he automatically made a mental adjustment for it. It was blowing from the harbor mouth toward the point at his back, so shouldn't have a huge effect.

He'd spent the prior morning loading twenty shells with a special blend of a more powerful charge to compensate for the velocity difference the silencer introduced, which had proved worthwhile when he was sighting it in. The higher-powered payload attenuated any distortion introduced by the device. He'd flattened the tips of each slug a little and carved an X into the top before filling the indentations with solder and filing them so there would be no danger of a jam. Nothing could ruin a well-planned assault like a faultily loading weapon, and so he'd spent hours on the task before taking the gun out and putting it through its paces.

He watched as the roaming sentry approached the seated guard, presumably to ask for a cigarette, because the seated man reached into his breast pocket and offered him one from his pack. *El Rey* regarded the two sentries through the scope, taking care to close his eyes while the seated man lit the other's smoke. It wouldn't do to ruin his night vision with the match's flare.

As the pair chatted lazily on the rear stone patio of the darkened house, *El Rey* gently squeezed the trigger. The standing man crumpled next to the seated guard, his chest exploding outward and onto his stunned partner; the fragmented slug having torn through his back, the shards exiting his front along with chunks of his pulmonary system and heart. *El Rey* caressed the trigger again, gently, as a lover might the receptive lips of his mate, and the seated man's throat blew onto the heavy stucco house's rear façade. That left the guard in front, who would be getting a little apprehensive within a few minutes when the roaming man didn't return on his appointed rounds.

El Rey waited patiently for the inevitable, and was rewarded after seven minutes by the sight of the third sentry rounding the corner of the house. Another well-placed shot took him down before he could draw his weapon. The assassin checked his watch and smiled to himself – in just ten minutes, the threat from the security force had been neutralized. He watched the grisly tableau for a few moments to ensure nobody was moving, then placed the rifle in the bottom of the boat before shrugging into a scuba harness. He double-checked the waterproof bag for the cell phone and two pistols before propelling himself backwards with a dull splash into the cold water of the bay.

It took him three minutes to swim the distance, and when he pulled himself onto the shallow beach in front of the house, he paused to unclasp the tank and remove the scuba rig, dropping it where he stood on the sand, along with his flippers. They, like the boat, would be recovered later that night by Victor's clean-up men, so he wasn't worried about leaving any traces.

He padded in his neoprene dive booties to the grass that separated the patio from the beach and extracted a silenced Beretta 92FS pistol from the bag. Quickly gliding to where the corpses lay, he put a muffled slug into each man's head, purely out of professional diligence. There was nothing more disruptive to a well-planned operation than a wounded man with a gun exhibiting second-wind heroics. The niggling housekeeping chores concluded, *El Rey* studied the locking mechanism of the rear pocket doors before fishing out a foot-long stainless steel strip that looked much like a ruler, which is what in fact it was, albeit modified with a jagged hook ground out of one end. He slid it carefully through the center section, and with an abrupt pull, opened the lock. Back into the bag it went, and he fished out the second pistol – an odd-looking gas-powered gun that fired a horse-tranquilizer dart.

The house blueprints Victor had sourced from the building department were still fresh in his mind as he stealthily ascended the stairs to where he knew the master bedroom was located. The neoprene soles of his booties made his steps silent – a fortunate by-product of his unfashionable outfit. As he drew nearer to the partially opened master bedroom door, his ears pricked up, listening for any tell-tale warning signs. Satisfied that the house was still, he pushed the door open, only to be rewarded with a creak from the hinges, corroded by the salt air.

The figure on the bed stirred at the sound and then lunged for the dresser. *El Rey* fired the dart gun left handed at him – the dart missed by a scant few inches and embedded itself into the pillow. The target swung around at him with a silenced pistol and began firing even as *El*

Rey made a split-second judgment call and charged him rather than shooting him. He ignored the white hot stab of pain that lanced through his upper leg as he hurled himself through the air at the prone, firing *El Chilango*, and within a heartbeat had dislodged the gun and was grappling with his left hand for the dart as he slammed his Beretta butt into the man's head with his right. The struggle was over in a matter of seconds, and the former cartel boss slumped into the mattress as the dart's soporific venom, stabbed into the side of his neck, found its way into his bloodstream.

El Rey lay still on top of the target for a few moments, assessing the throbbing pain from his thigh. He felt blood seeping from the wound – but it wasn't spurting, which meant the projectile hadn't hit an artery. Still, it was bad, and the pain was significant. After looking around the room, he rose and limped to the master closet and flicked on the light. His eyes scanned the rows of neatly hanging clothes until they alighted on a bathrobe with a sash for cinching the waist. He pulled the fabric strip loose, then pulled drawers open until he found some white cotton undershirts, all folded in neat little parcels. He grabbed one and tied it in place using the sash, studying the makeshift bandage with acerbic satisfaction. It would do until he could get medical attention.

He returned to the dark bedroom and reached into the waterproof bag dangling from his dive belt to retrieve the cell phone. Peering at the target's inert form on the bed, he pressed a speed dial number. Victor's voice answered.

"Front door. Two minutes. I've been hit, so I'll need a medic as soon as possible," *El Rey* whispered.

"Hit? How bad?"

"Small caliber pistol clipped me in the leg. Be here in two minutes, and send the cleanup crew to get the gear and the boat."

"I'll have the lads push the bodies into the bay as well, if yah don't mind," Victor suggested.

"No worries," *El Rey* answered, in the ubiquitous manner he'd heard used countless times by the locals since his arrival.

Gimping over to the bed, he lifted *El Chilango* by both arms and dragged him roughly into the hall and then down the stairs. The man would be out cold for two hours, he knew, and when he awoke his head would feel like someone had hammered it with a board, which wasn't far from the truth, given the gashes the pistol had left, the blood already coagulating and crusting where it had streamed down his face.

On the ground floor, he slid the inert body to the front entrance foyer and watched through the side window for the vehicle. Twenty seconds later, he saw an outline pull up. He swung the door open, to be greeted by the sight of Victor trotting from the black delivery van they'd arranged for the evening's festivities. He took a hard look at *El Rey*, standing in the doorway with blood oozing through the T-shirt affixed to his leg, and then wordlessly went to *El Chilango* and began dragging him to the back of the van. *El Rey* limped over, helped get the target into the back, and climbed in after him.

"Get me a doctor. I think the bullet passed clean through, but I need to get cauterized and stitched up," he instructed.

"I've got a call in. Should hear back any minute. Let's do that before we hit the warehouse, shall we? I can secure our friend here so if he wakes up in the interim he can't get up to any mischief," Victor said.

"Good. Let's go."

Victor closed the back doors and ran around to the driver's seat. In the blink of an eye they were headed down the carefully manicured street, bound for the main road. Victor was just turning onto the larger artery when his cell rang.

"Yeah. I need it now. Ten minutes out, maybe fifteen. Your shop? No worries," Victor said, and hung up. He leaned towards the rear compartment. "We'll swing by his office. He's pretty good for this kinda thing," Victor assured *El Rey*.

They drove through Sydney until they reached a rough-looking section, the buildings shabby and tattooed with graffiti. Victor pulled to the curb in front of a small storefront featuring photos of yellow Labrador puppies bounding about in a grassy meadow. A short, bald, overweight man stood in the doorway, fumbling for keys to open it. *El Rey* looked up when Victor eased the rear van doors open and gingerly slid himself out and onto the sidewalk, waving off the unspoken offer of assistance. He looked at the little man and then at the shop window, then glared at Victor.

"A veterinarian?" he whispered.

"Bloke's top shelf. Have you running marathons in no time. Does all my sensitive jobs. No worries, mate. Nigel, come over and let's get our man here inside," Victor called out.

"I can make it. Let's just get this over with," *El Rey* hissed through clenched teeth.

He limped to the door, which Nigel had finally opened after locating the correct key.

"Name's Nigel. Doctor Nigel to you," he said, offering his hand.

"I'm shot in the leg. Let's clean it and sew it up," *El Rey* said, moving inside.

They walked to the back of the shop, where there was a small exam room with a stainless steel table in the center. Nigel flicked on the lights while Victor returned to the van to shackle their captive.

"Best get you up on the table, then. Let's see what we've got here," Nigel said, donning a disposable surgical apron and mask. He turned to where *El Rey* now lay and peered at the wound. "I'll have to cut away your party dress, if you can deal with the loss."

"Do what you have to do."

Nigel expertly untied the dressing and snipped away the neoprene, cutting the entire wetsuit leg off just below the groin and pulling it off. Blood seeped slowly from the holes on both sides of *El Rey*'s thigh. Nigel moved to the medicine cabinet, filled a syringe with Novocain and injected it carefully on the edges of the wound, finishing by squirting some directly in. The pain receded, replaced by sweet numbness.

Nigel swabbed the bullet hole and then used a pair of forceps to examine it.

"You got lucky. Missed the bone, and nothing major hit other than muscle. It'll smart for a bit, but I can stitch you up and you'll be a new man in no time," he assured *El Rey*. "The slug passed clean through so I'll just dump some antiseptic in, give you some antibiotics, some orange juice, and do a bit of sewing. Job done, mate."

"Give me two more syringes of the anesthetic, too. I need to do some more work tonight, and it's helping."

"Too right, then. Couple of sticks of 'feel good' to go. Can do. Now let's close you, shall we?"

Fifteen minutes later, the wound had been tended. Nigel sprayed both stitched areas with a metallic silver spray and stood back to admire his handiwork. *El Rey* sat up and began drinking a bottle of orange juice Nigel had brought him. The vet handed him two bottles of pills and two full syringes.

"That there's iron, for rebuilding your red blood cells, and that's doxycycline. Take one every eight hours for ten days. The numbing juice should be good for an hour or two each go. I'd remember to use alcohol to sterilize the area before you inject, and lose the syringe after using it once. Don't want to introduce any more germs than you need to, right? Now, if you'll take down your suit, I need to give you a shot in the bum so you don't die of sepsis."

El Rey pulled down the zipper at the front of his neck and obliged. The injection in his ass hurt almost as much as the gunshot had. The pain subsided after thirty seconds, and he realized it was hot in the suit, so he left it unzipped when he pulled it back up.

"Are we done?" Victor asked, coming back in after eavesdropping on the discussion.

"Yep. He should rest for a few days. Call me if there's any complications, like high fever or obvious signs of infection." Nigel gave a wan smile. He fixed *El Rey* with a good-natured gaze, his eyes twinkling with merriment. "You'll have a little pucker there, once you heal, to show the ladies. Cut out the stitches in seven days. Could do it in four, but seven's better if you're going to be walking around on it, which I imagine you will."

"Thanks, Doc. You're a dream," Victor said, shaking Nigel's hand. *El Rey* silently walked out of the room towards the front of the store, anxious to deliver his captive to the warehouse and fulfill his contract.

He was ready to get to work.

CHAPTER 14

Outside the warehouse, the streets were empty, save for a mottled, scrawny cat nosing its way down the sidewalk in search of edible bounty. It paused at a rubbish container thirty yards from the sliding metal door, sniffing for anything to feed on. It looked up, startled by the van swinging round the corner, and quickly darted off in search of safer pickings.

Victor got out of the van and slid the door open before driving inside. He killed the engine, then returned to the door to close it.

El Rey stopped him. "Let's get him out of the back, and I'll take it from here. I'll call you when I'm done."

Victor eyed him. "It's your party. You can play whatever music yah like," he said, strolling to the rear of the van and opening the doors. *El Chilango* lay, still unconscious, with duct tape over his mouth, his legs bound with it and his wrists cuffed together in front of him. Victor rooted around in his pocket and wordlessly handed *El Rey* the key to the cuffs.

They dragged the ex-cartel chief out and dumped him unceremoniously onto the floor.

Victor took a quick scan of the workspace. "Everything yah asked for is here. There's some clothes, the Sony, and all the rest." He grinned, looking cadaverous under the harsh fluorescent lighting. "Just ring me, and I'll be by in ten. I hafta go attend to making sure the clean-up boys did their job and didn't miss anything. Good luck, mate," he said, then climbed into the driver's seat and started the van. It swung back out onto the street, and *El Rey* closed the large door behind it, latching it in place so they wouldn't be disturbed.

He took a good look at his prisoner and hobbled to the table in the corner, unfolding the clothes he'd left there before changing into them. Once he was done, he studied the items scattered around the table and moved to a wickedly sharp combat knife and a pair of surgical scissors. He'd set the camera up later. He wanted to get everything right for his performance art debut, and he had a very specific idea about how his project would begin.

El Chilango came to with a start and instantly began shivering as he registered the cold cement floor against his naked body. He shook his head in an effort to clear it, tried to move his arms and legs. It was no good. He'd been bound. Out of the periphery of his vision, he made out movement, and he craned his neck to see what fresh hell he'd fallen into. A young Latino man stepped into view.

"I see the smelling salts worked. How are you feeling?" *El Rey* asked in Spanish.

"What are you doing? What do you want? Money? I have a lot of it…," *El Chilango* said.

"I'm glad to hear that. Hopefully you have a current will, too. It would be a shame if it all went to waste, no?"

El Chilango grimaced. "I can make you rich. Anything you want, I can give you."

"That's an attractive offer. Really. It's not every day someone offers to make all my dreams come true," *El Rey* mused, walking over to a tripod where a small video camera was positioned. He looked through the screen and adjusted the height a little and then, satisfied, pulled a balaclava from his pocket and pulled the knit mask over his head. He depressed the record button and verified that it was operating correctly before moving back to *El Chilango*.

"What the fuck are you doing? Did you hear me? I can give you any amount of money you want. Any. A million dollars. Five million. Ten. Anything. Just say the number and I can make it so..." *El Chilango* was panicking after seeing the mask – he realized what was happening. "Please. You don't have to do this. I can make you rich for life–"

His protestations were cut off by the clanking of chain feeding through an overhead electric winch mounted to one of the crossbeams. The motor whined, and he felt pressure on his ankles as it slowly started lifting him off the floor.

"Oh God, no. Please. Name a number. Anything..."

Once he was suspended upside down, he began shrieking and howling in stark fear, squirming and struggling in a futile effort to get free. The motor stopped when his head was three feet off the floor. He spun gently in a circle from his efforts, slowly returning to the central position, his face looking in fear at the camera.

El Rey checked the image through the viewfinder one last time and nodded, satisfied with the composition.

"It's so hard to create an interesting film. Sustaining the drama, capturing the pathos, making the audience feel like they're involved...," *El Rey* lamented.

"Let me down. You don't have to do this. Please," the cartel boss whimpered, saliva flecking from his mouth with every word.

El Rey moved to the table and donned a clear plastic raincoat, taking care to snap up the front of it. When he turned to face *El Chilango*, he looked at his watch and ignited the tip of the welding torch he held in one hand with the long-handled fireplace lighter he held in the other. *El Chilango*'s eyes grew wide.

"So you can give me any amount of money I want?" *El Rey* asked.

"Yes. Anything. You'll be rich. I can make you rich. Millions," he pleaded, beginning to cry as he saw the blue flame and understood the implications of the camera and his complete nudity.

"Tell me. What does it cost to bring a twelve-year-old ballerina back to life? How much is a little girl's life worth? What's the going rate?"

El Chilango struggled to process the question, to make sense of what was being asked, and then awareness dawned on him.

"Noooooooooo..." Urine streamed down his bare chest as he lost control of his bodily functions out of raw terror.

El Rey set the torch on the table, pushing the surgical rotary saw aside to make room, and picked up a red suede muzzle designed to keep victims silent that Victor had gotten from a bondage store. With a final glance at his victim, he approached *El Chilango*, humming a song he'd heard that morning. Waltzing Matilda. For whatever reason it had stayed with him, the melody catchy in an odd way.

Shortly thereafter he began his first film appearance in earnest.

Three hours later, Victor's phone rang.

"It's done. Dispose of the remains and hose down the shop. Thanks for everything," *El Rey* said, before hanging up. He'd settled up with Victor earlier, so there were 'no worries' in that respect.

He studied the three small video cassettes and labeled them one through three with a fine-tip marker, then slipped them into his pocket before turning off the work area lights. He was glad he wouldn't have to clean up after the mess – it was all he'd been able to do to avoid getting soaked with blood in the end. The dismemberment and cauterization had been gratuitous, but then again his little cinematic epic was intended for a very specific audience. He suspected what it lacked in finesse would be made up by the subject matter. He'd stretched things out as long as they would go and, fortunately, *El Chilango* had been healthy and strong.

It was amazing the amount of abuse the human body could take and still keep functioning.

Still, when all was said and done, nothing lasted forever.

El Rey limped down the street, still humming, his leg starting to throb but still largely numb from the two injections. He'd get out of town in the late morning and be back home within twenty hours of taking off, with any luck at all.

A few minutes later, he saw the lights of his hotel and exhaled with relief at the thought of a few hours of rest.

It had been a long day.

The Qantas first class lounge was mostly empty so *El Rey* had the area he was sitting in all to himself. He nibbled on some cashews and drank some more orange juice while gazing through the window at the huge airplanes landing as he waited for his flight to be called. His leg hurt like hell, but he'd be fine. He didn't want to take any pain medicine but reconciled to perhaps availing himself of the expensive free alcohol that flowed like water in the first class cabin. It wasn't like he would need to be in total control while thirty-nine thousand feet over the Pacific Ocean. It would be safe to violate his prohibition against alcohol in cases of emergency. It was, after all, for legitimate medicinal reasons.

Fortunately, his seat pod folded flat into a bed, so he would be able to sleep for much of the way if he had any luck at all. The trip over had been relatively smooth and he was hopeful that it would be equally uneventful on the return across the Pacific as well. His English was more than good enough to follow the dialogue in the in-flight films, so he could catch a movie or two while waiting to drift off. He never watched TV or movies back home, so it was a guilty pleasure he planned to indulge while aloft.

The *El Chilango* contract would be the last of the year for him. He wanted to recuperate from the shooting, and also not be overly available to any of the cartels – preferring to select the assignments he accepted with care. He wouldn't get to the point where he could command millions for a hit by being open to every job thrown his way. He intended to only take the truly challenging sanctions, thereby creating a reputation as a man who could do the impossible – the court of last resort when only the best would do. That would take as much stagecraft and pomp as it would competent execution. Everything in the end was a performance, and if he managed his career correctly he would soon be the star of center stage when it came to headline-making assassinations.

The loudspeaker announced his flight and an attractive young redheaded Australian woman came to assist him with the wheelchair that sat waiting in a corner. He'd told the airline that he was disabled, a diving accident, and the staff had been more than accommodating. As the perky airline worker pushed him to the gate, he again remarked at how clean everything was in Sydney. It wasn't home, of course, but Australia certainly had its charms. He could understand the appeal as a retirement destination, although for the life of him he couldn't figure out what the people were saying half the time.

Once onboard, he stowed his overnight bag and settled in for the long journey ahead. He had booked a seat at the very front of the 747, with nobody in front of him, and he hoped the section would be only a third full, as it had been on the way over.

Eventually the door closed and he saw, with satisfaction, that nobody else was in his row. Thankfully, he'd be left in peace. *El Rey* plugged his headphones into the center console and adjusted the channel to the classical station, then thumbed through the onboard magazine to see what had been selected for his viewing pleasure by the attentive entertainment concierge at Qantas. A grinning stewardess came down the aisle and offered him a glass of Veuve Clicquot champagne, which he gratefully accepted while returning the woman's smile. She brought it promptly, along with a porcelain bowl of warm, mixed nuts, and reminded him to simply ask if he had any other requests or needs. He leaned back in his seat with a weary sigh as he sipped the bubbly ambrosia from the glass flute, and peered through the window while the plane backed away from the gate. Shaking out an iron pill and antibiotic, he washed them down with the last of the elixir, and before long the massive aircraft was lumbering down the runway and up into the cold morning light.

ABOUT THE AUTHOR

Russell Blake lives full time on the Pacific coast of Mexico. He is the acclaimed author of the thrillers: *Fatal Exchange*, *The Geronimo Breach*, *Zero Sum*, *The Delphi Chronicle* trilogy (*The Manuscript*, *The Tortoise and the Hare*, and *Phoenix Rising*), *King of Swords*, *Night of the Assassin*, *The Voynich Cypher*, *Revenge of the Assassin*, *Return of the Assassin*, *Blood of the Assassin*, *Silver Justice*, *JET*, *JET II – Betrayal*, *JET III – Vengeance*, *JET IV – Reckoning*, *JET V - Legacy*, *Upon a Pale Horse*, *BLACK*, and *BLACK is Back*.

Non-fiction novels include the international bestseller *An Angel With Fur* (animal biography) and *How To Sell A Gazillion eBooks (while drunk, high or incarcerated)* – a joyfully vicious parody of all things writing and self-publishing related.

"Capt." Russell enjoys writing, fishing, playing with his dogs, collecting and sampling tequila, and waging an ongoing battle against world domination by clowns.

Sign up for e-mail updates about new Russell Blake releases

http://russellblake.com/contact/mailing-list